Fic
G

BURGUNDY FARM COUNTRY DAY SCHOOL

LUCITA

"Lucita tried in vain to catch them in her quick, brown hands"

LUCITA

A CHILD'S STORY OF OLD MEXICO

By RUTH GAINES

With pictures by
MAGINEL WRIGHT ENRIGHT

RAND McNALLY & COMPANY

CHICAGO　　　　　　　　　　　　　　　　　NEW YORK

Copyright, 1913, by
RUTH GAINES

𝔗𝔥𝔢 𝔑𝔞𝔫𝔡-𝔐𝔠𝔑𝔞𝔩𝔩𝔶 𝔓𝔯𝔢𝔰𝔰
Chicago

Á Lucita mia

THE FOREWORD

LUCITA, as the story will tell you, was born on one of Our Lady's days, the day of Our Lady of Light. That is how she got her name. And she was born not so far from the United States, in what the Mexicans call the United States of Mexico. Mexico used to be a province of Spain, and in many ways it is like Spain to-day. They speak Spanish there; and Lucita is the Spanish word for Little Light. Lucita, though it is longer, is really short for Luz.

Lucita is a real girl, a girl whom I know. I hope you will like what I tell you of her, because I like her so well.

RUTH GAINES.

ACKNOWLEDGMENTS

My first thanks are due to my friend, Miss Georgia Willis Read, who went with me to Mexico to make the acquaintance of my little heroine. In fact, it was she who really found her for me. In the cool of a summer afternoon she spied her with her mother beside the haunted fountain. The open gateway framed a picture so lovely that it lured us again and again, until one day we were asked across the threshold into Lucita's world. Miss Read has helped me not only by her inspiration but in more practical ways as well by taking the photographs which have served as a background for the story, and by her helpful criticism throughout.

To R. P. Conkling, who has made a special study of Mexican folk songs, I owe the charming music of Petra's lullaby. For careful reading of proof and notes I am indebted to my father, a scholar and a teacher of long experience, and for their final revision to Mrs. Fanny Hale Gardiner, who is an acknowledged authority on Spain and Mexico and a writer of distinction. To the artist, Mrs. Enright, for her sympathetic interpretation, and to all these friends, I desire to express my thanks.

RUTH GAINES.

New York, January, 1913.

THE CONTENTS

	PAGE
The Foreword	vii
Acknowledgments	viii
The Illustrations	x
I. THE QUEEN'S GARDEN	1
II. A-MARKETING	10
III. THE LADY OF THE FOUNTAIN	17
IV. FRANCISCA'S DAY	27
V. THE EASTER BIRDS	34
VI. THE COMING OF PAPA	40
VII. SAN ANGEL	46
VIII. THE SUGAR MILL	51
IX. THE CAVE OF WATERS	55
X. A LETTER	63
XI. THE RAID	68
XII. THE RUINS OF ATLAN	74
XIII. AT THE FORGE	78

THE CONTENTS

	PAGE
XIV. THE PRESIDENT'S HUNT	87
XV. LITTLE BROTHER	92
Petra's Lullaby	100
Notes	101
A Reading List	110
A Guide to Pronunciation	112
Suggestions to Teachers	114

THE ILLUSTRATIONS

FULL PAGE

"*Lucita tried in vain to catch them in her quick, brown hands*" Frontispiece

FACING PAGE

"*She had seen the special ghost of the house float with flying veils along the gallery*"	1
"'*We want a basket with a cover*'"	15
"*A merry cavalcade they made, riding down the street*"	31
At the door of the sugar house	51
The two girls sat in a hammock and talked	70
"*They began to row over the black waters of the lake*"	83
There on Petra's knee lay Little Brother, fast asleep	92

TEXT

PAGE

"*She was dipping up water in her little green pot and pouring it over the grateful plants*"	4
"'*Will you buy flowers?*'"	11
"'*How do you like this?*' inquired Aunt Stasia"	18
"*A group of curious Indian children*"	32
"*Boys with toys arranged like huge bouquets of flowers cried their wares at every corner*"	35
The Hacienda	44
Great sheaves of sugar cane were bound to the backs of mules	46
Sugar rick	52
A sugar house	53
The Indian huts	58
"*Vicente was the potter we went to see*"	65

xii THE ILLUSTRATIONS

PAGE

In the potter's village 66
A potter of Las Palmillas 67
Making tortillas 69
"Those Indians who were not busy . . . pressed closer" 90
In the market 97

"She had seen the special ghost of the house float with flying veils along the gallery". Page 1

LUCITA

A CHILD'S STORY OF OLD MEXICO

I

THE QUEEN'S GARDEN

ALL night the wind had blown down from the northern barrier of mountains. All night it had whirled the fine dust of the street in drifts upon the red-tiled floor, and clanked against the rickety shutters. It had rattled the tiles on the roof until Lucita (as "Little Light" is called in Spanish) thought all the ghosts in Rosario were dancing above her head. Indeed, as she looked out once into the deserted *patio*, dimly lighted by the moon, she had seen the special ghost of the house float with flying veils along the gallery. Oh, yes, they had a ghost, a Lady of the Fountain, Doña Marina by name. Lucita could have told you all about her, by daytime, when she was not frightened. Last night she had not wanted to tell any one but mamma, and to run into her room and cuddle close up to her, and forget the howling wind.

With the dawn, the wind died away. The morning broke through a brownish haze over the brown valley. The cracked bells of the cathedral across the street clacked and jangled. But Lucita slept through it all. Lucita's mamma pulled the sheets a little closer as she stood looking down at her, and bent to kiss her forehead. It was a pretty forehead, round and smooth, and fringed with dark brown curls. Beneath it, long lashes lay very still against cheeks that looked like nothing so much as wild-rose leaves. At least, that is what mamma thought as she kissed her and left her to finish her nap.

After such a night of storm there was much to be done in the dilapidated house in which Lucita and her mamma and her Aunt Anastasia lived. They had not been there long. A year ago they had had a much grander home in the City of Mexico, with papa. Then papa went away, and mamma, for some reason that eight-year-old Lucita did not understand, moved to Rosario, to this old, bare house. To be sure, it could not be called bare any longer; in the front room were shelves stacked high with embroideries and drawn work of linen; beneath long counters gleamed old jewelry and precious stones, pocketbooks, belts and cases of carved leather, and trinkets of wonderful colored glass. The cracked walls were hidden by blue and gold brocades from Japan, brought across the sea hundreds of years ago by the rich Spanish nobles when Mexico was a province of Spain. Pictures, too, there were, done by artists who loved to paint the life of the country in street and market place. Opening from this room were two others, one containing potteries, famous wares of Talavera and of Puebla, in curiously wrought patterns of blue and green, the other overflowing with Indian blankets that glowed against wall and floor like Joseph's coat of many colors.

Some of the articles Lucita's mother was trying to sell came from her old home; some she bought when she decided to open a store and make enough money for herself and her little daughter to live on while her husband worked in the United States to win back their lost fortunes. For Rosario was a city with a history, and many tourists with money to spend visited it during the winter time, which was always summer there.

So it was that Doña María (as Lucita's mother was called) and Aunt Anastasia were up betimes this morning, sweeping and shaking and dusting. To-day an important tourist party was expected, no less a person than the Austrian Minister to Mexico and a visiting prince of his imperial house. Out in the gallery, meantime, old Petra was rattling her earthenware pots, and directing her small assistant, Alejandro, in his task of fanning to a glow the charcoal in the braziers which formed her stove. Soon the pleasant fragrance of coffee filled the court, and the hissing of the frying pan told that the *tortillas* were being made. It was then that Lucita awoke.

With a spring she was out of bed, across the inner court, and splashing in the fountain that served as her bath. The sparrows, who wanted their morning dip, too, flew off at her approach, but came back to settle contentedly on the rim, where Lucita tried in vain to catch them in her quick, brown hands. Tia Stasia arrived presently to stop her play, and to rub her dry and slip her into her clothes. Then Lucita was ready to sit down to breakfast, as hungry and as happy as a little brown sparrow herself.

Mamma looked up with a smile as she took her place at the table. "Good morning, Little Light," she said. "You are late in shining to-day. Your plants out in the *patio* are missing you, and so is Chiquito, too."

At once Lucita's face showed she was sorry. She looked at the thrush's cage, still covered by its green bag, and at the flowers, dusty and thirsty, on the balustrade of the court.

"I know, mamma," she answered; "but it was such a night. Even the Lady of the Fountain could not sleep. But I will hurry, truly I will."

And so Lucita did. It was not long till she was dipping up water in her little green pot and pouring it over the grateful plants. Afterwards she sprinkled the tiled floor, and her bare feet as well, with the cooling spray. Then she unhung Chiquito's cage. "Poor Chiquito," she called him, and Chiquito seemed to understand, for he cocked his head on one side and answered with an injured little note. Presently, though, he must have felt that he had nothing to complain of, for he swung from perch to perch of his clean cage, in the shade of the orange tree, and trilled forth a wonderful song.

"*She was dipping up water in her little green pot and pouring it over the grateful plants*"

Usually after the morning tasks Tia Stasia—who really wasn't very much grown up, after all—bore Lucita away to some quiet nook for the reading lesson or the story that served as a lesson each day. But this morning she was too busy. Little girls were in the way on a tourists' day. Lucita stole happily into the garden, her refuge from such intruders. A beautiful place that garden was. Through an iron gate you looked first far, far down a path shaded by mango trees and flecked with sunshine. At the end the sunshine fell full on the marble basin of a fountain. To left and right other paths branched off into tangles of coffee bushes and roses, and you knew not what, until you had run down each separate path to see. Somewhere, high up in the tree tops, birds were always singing. You could hear them even at the gate. But at the gate you did not pause long; the wicket opened smoothly, and there you were.

To-day Lucita ran straight down the main alley to the fountain, and turned to the right. Before her lay a lake, with steps leading invitingly down to the water, and ducks that seemed to know Lucita, by the way they swam to her feet. From the pocket of her pink apron she drew the crumbs Petra had given her, and scattered them broadcast. Then such a quacking as arose, and such a flurry of wings and legs and long, yellow bills! One poor little brown duck, set upon by all the others, swam away with loud quacks.

"Oh, shame!" cried Lucita, and ran along the edge and coaxed it until it, too, had a share of the treat she had brought.

As she skipped away from the lake some of the flock still

followed her, waddling clumsily along the walk. But she soon left them behind. High up on the wall, at the farther side of the garden, stood a little *mirador*, or pavilion. Inside was a broad concrete bench, and from it a lovely view of a little winding valley could be seen. Underneath the pavilion was a kind of cellarway, where the gardeners kept their tools: long, sickle-shaped knives for cutting and pruning, hoes, and spades. Among them, a bundle of forgotten and faded flags leaned against the wall. Here was Lucita's castle. Here, in imagination, she flung her banners from the bastions, and peopled her dungeon with knights and prisoners. It was not so very many years ago—not longer than Petra could remember—that these same banners had in truth fluttered from the walls, to announce to the city of Rosario that the Empress Carlota was spending her summer there. She had fed the ducks in the lake, just as Lucita had done, and walked down the same garden paths. Lucita knew how she had come from a far-away country to rule over Mexico, and knew, too, that she had liked to sit in the *mirador* and look down the crumpled valley to the blue mountains, behind which lay the blue sea, and her home. Indeed, Little Light was the Empress Carlota to-day!

As she sat thus in her castle she was suddenly aware of footsteps, and looked up to meet the square gaze of a pair of brown eyes nearly on a level with her own. A gold-braided visor shaded them, and a gold-braided uniform of blue completed the dress of the small personage who stood before her.

The empress, expecting instead white-trousered Alejandro with some message from the house, stared back.

"I beg your pardon," said the boy in hesitating Spanish, "but who are you?"

"I am the Empress Carlota—that is, I am Lucita de Alarcón. And who are you?"

"I am a prince, but I am very tired of being a prince, and I should just like to come in and talk to you. You are very pretty," he added. "If you are an empress, I think you might do for me to play with, might you not?"

"Do!" echoed Lucita, looking with astonishment at this really-truly prince, who had evidently strayed away from the rest of his party. "My papa is a Mexican *caballero*, and my mamma is an *Americana*," she explained. "In our countries we have no princes. If you're not an Indian, you're good enough to play with anybody."

The boy regarded her curiously. "All right," he said. "I remember; in your countries you have presidents, and all the people may be presidents, is it not so? Anyway, you are the first person I ever met who did not bow to me, and I like it. I think I'll come in."

Then began a morning Lucita—and I suspect the prince, too—never forgot. Together they held the castle against invading armies of gardeners; together they picked the red berries of the coffee and spread them in the sun to dry. They even got out the old boat on the lake, and the prince rowed Lucita over to the little islands midway between the shores. Lucita told him about Chiquito, and the Lady of the Fountain, and the empress who used to live here before Mexico became a republic or had a President Diaz.

At this the boy broke in. "I, too, know of that empress," he said. "She was an Austrian, like me. Your people killed her emperor and drove her away."

"I did not know that," said Lucita, slowly; "only that the Empress Carlota lived in my garden and loved it. She was young then, and happy, and beautiful."

The prince looked anxiously into his playmate's clouded face. "Come," he said, "it all happened very long ago." He hurried on to tell her how he had visited President Diaz in his castle at Chapultepec only yesterday. He told her, too, of his life in Austria, of his little sisters, the princesses, and of their sedate little games.

"They play with dolls, and they would like to run up and down these paths with hoops. Do you like dolls?"

Lucita hung her head. All of a sudden she wanted very much to please this truly prince. "No," she faltered, "I—I don't care for dolls. I make up my dolls out of my head, I think. And I like to climb trees, and I play with the ducks. I wouldn't do for a princess, you see."

They had paused beneath a tree tufted with feathery, pink tassels. "What do you call this tree?" the boy asked gravely.

"Angels' Hair," she answered.

"Will you please get me a tassel?" he asked. "I cannot reach them."

It was while Lucita was perched in one of the low, spreading branches that the prince's attendants came in sight. With some anxiety and a good deal of laughter they surrounded him, and would have borne him away.

"One moment," the prince protested. "I must thank my hostess."

And as Lucita, now quite abashed, slid to the ground, he took the delicate sprays from her hands with a low bow.

"You are my princess, remember," he said, and so was gone.

II

A-MARKETING

IT was not every day, by any means, that Lucita had a live prince to play with. Indeed, her little playmates were nearly all girls. There were Pancha de Herrera's brother and Dick Merton, to be sure, but Dick was a whole two years older, and Pablo,—well, he was just Pancha's brother. Petra's little boy, Alejandro, did not count. You could not play with an Indian. His place was to run errands and to take care of the drove of donkeys Doña María let to the *turistas* to ride. When he had time, he also went to school.

"I think," Lucita confided to her mother the morning after the prince's visit, "I think the prince is the only boy I ever really did like. Please, couldn't you fix that I have a brother one day, just like him?"

Lucita's mother smiled. "It may be—some day."

"Some day soon, please," begged Lucita. And from that time began her dream of "Little Brother," a little brother who would play with her always, and always be her prince.

But not every day was even a play day for Lucita. She, as well as the grown-ups, had her share of household tasks. This very morning a knocking at the gate interrupted her talk with her mother. She ran to open it.

Outside stood an Indian woman, barefooted, with a blue shawl wound around her shoulders.

A-MARKETING

"Good morning, *niñita*," she said. "Will you buy some flowers?" She threw back the blue and white fringe of her shawl to show the bunches of yellow roses and pansies and forget-me-nots on her tray. "They are very cheap, *niñita*."

"How much?" returned Lucita, as she smelled the fresh roses. "How much for these?"

"Ten cents," said Catalina with a smile. Every morning she came with her flowers, and every morning the same bargaining took place.

"No," said Lucita, as she did every day; "that is too much. I will give you five."

"Five!" exclaimed Catalina. "Why, it does not pay for the picking, let alone bringing them. But I will sell them for eight cents—to you."

"*Will you buy flowers?*"

"Seven cents I will give," said Lucita firmly. And so the flowers were bought. Afterwards she placed them in a deep bowl in the hallway, where they glowed like a spot of sunlight against the dark walls.

Presently from the kitchen came Petra, with two baskets, one large and one small, on her arm.

"It is time to go to the market. Are you not coming, Lucita?" she said.

"In a moment," Lucita answered. "I will get my purse and come."

Down the narrow street, already glaring white in the sunlight, they went, Lucita skipping in advance. About the door of the convent the children were gathering for the morning session. Farther on, the girls of the public school sat on the sidewalk, or bought sweetmeats from a vender, who had set up his tray of candies in the shade. Several of them called *"Buenos dias"* to Lucita as she passed. A few doors beyond she and Petra stopped at the bakery. *"Panadería el Vapor"* it was called; and in truth a steam from many appetizing breads and rolls arose from the dark interior. Not many customers were in the shop at this hour. Earlier, at sunrise, the place swarmed like a beehive; great baskets piled high with "kisses," "potatoes," "crescents," "bread of egg," and a score of other fancy varieties were brought out hot from the ovens; the shelves were heaped with them, the counters overflowed, and men, women, and children filled their smaller baskets from the bountiful supply. Now everything was swept clean; on the shelves were only little packets of salt, boxes of matches, bars of soap, and candles, which the baker also sold. But in response to Petra's greeting he brought out from a drawer the rolls and the long, narrow loaves he had saved for her. She placed them in her basket, and with a pleasant *"Adios,"* followed after Lucita, now far down the street.

For Lucita was in a hurry to meet Carmen Carrillo in the Plaza, and take her along to the market. Under the deep shade of the plane trees that lined the walks of the tiny park she found her waiting. Others were sitting there, too; white-clad Indians, American tourists, Juan the newsboy, the druggist, the linen draper, and many whom Lucita knew. The sun was hot this January morning, and they felt the need of rest. Besides, it was nearly time for the clattering trams and the coaches to start for the station, to meet the morning train. Lucita sat down on the bench with Carmen to wait for the great event. Presently the huge, lumbering stage, with much cracking of whips, set off. A tooting of horns followed, the tram drivers' warning to clear the way. The whips flew out, the mules strained, and the cars rattled at a gallop up the cobbled street.

After the excitement was over, Lucita turned to Carmen's nurse. Carmen was the governor's daughter, and far more carefully guarded than Lucita.

"May Carmen come with me to the market to-day?" she asked. "I want to buy some baskets and some dishes for Pancha's birthday next week, and I need her to help me. She knows so very much more about dolls' dishes than I. Petra is with me," she continued. "I am to meet her at the 'Light of Day.'"

"Indeed, I may come," cried Miss Carmen, quite ignoring the nurse. "May I not?" she added eagerly.

"Go along, little tease," Antonia answered. "I am quite comfortable to wait for you here."

Now, the "Light of Day" was a grocery, situated at one corner of the marketplace. When Lucita and Carmen reached it the grocer was just chopping up a hard, white cone of sugar, the last article on Petra's list. Whack! whack! went the hatchet, and the children watched with fascinated eyes as the flakes of sugar fell. Presently the grocer paused, scooped these flakes into a paper, gave each end a deft twirl, and dropped the whole into Lucita's basket.

"Sweets to the sweet," he laughed.

The entrance to the market was crowded this morning, as it always was on a Thursday. In booths men were selling ice cream and pink lemonade; a merry-go-round stood at one side, and as Lucita and Carmen passed, the music started and the horses whirled happy little Indian riders round and round; on the ground women sat before piles of peanuts, and sugar cones, and hot *tamales* "baked while you wait." Through the jostling people Petra guided her young charges, until they came to the potters' booths. Here, spread on mats, was a wonderful array; tiny braziers no bigger than Lucita's hand, but made to hold a real fire, for all that; cups and jugs of fluted glass, tinted like flowers, half an inch high; little sets of red-lacquered gourds for bowls, nests of brown-glazed cooking dishes, and, most fascinating of all, water jugs topped by little, inverted cups. And each cup bore a name!

"Oh, oh!" cried Lucita in delight. "I never saw these in the market before."

"That is because you were not looking," returned the more practical Carmen, selecting a jug with *Pancha* stenciled on it in lines of blue and red. "See these *ollas;* they have names, too. Yes, here is a Pancha, and it just fits this *brasero.*" She picked up a red brazier and placed a round-bottomed jar on top.

"'We want a basket with a cover'"

"It needs only a fan to fan the fire, doesn't it?" said Lucita. "I know where those are, anyway. But I'm going to get some of these lovely glass dishes first."

The little packages in the basket mounted higher at each turn. And meantime Petra, with a patient air, paid the reckless bills. When you really want anything, you have no chance at a bargain!

At last she guided the children toward the inner square of the market, where the vegetables were sold. For the family needed fresh lettuce and peas and peppers this morning, and she had no mind "to let every housewife in Rosario have first choice." Besides, the flower stalls were here, too, and the basket booths, where the children had yet other treasures to buy. Baskets, little and big, swung from the low roofs; they peeped from out-of-the-way corners among piles of rope, mats for the floor, heaps of colored beans, hempen bags, and the hundred and one things that a basket vender sells.

Carmen was spokesman. "We want," she said, "a basket with a cover, just big enough to hold these." She pointed to the bundles of toys.

"But of what shape, and of what color?" asked the clerk with a smile. "There are so many kinds."

"With a crimson border."

"And with lids that open and shut," added Lucita, "like —like a butterfly's wings."

Presto! it was set down before her, woven of fine grasses, tinted like a rainbow, and all for ten cents.

To Lucita and Carmen it seemed a marvel. They could

hardly wait to get to the Plaza, where they packed their dishes inside. Nor did it seem as if they could wait a whole week for Pancha's birthday party, before they gave it to her.

"Who shall keep it?" asked Carmen.

Lucita looked at it longingly. She would have liked to sleep with it beside her bed every night, and to unpack it every day. But—

"You," she said. "You care more for dolls than I."

III

THE LADY OF THE FOUNTAIN

"LUCITA, *Lucita mia!*" It was Aunt Anastasia who called, in a sweet, high-pitched voice that floated down from the roof to the Court of the Fountain, where Lucita still lingered to feed her sparrows. By it, Lucita knew that a morning of lessons had at last arrived. Not that she dreaded them; no, indeed. She ran quickly up the steep stairs leading from the court to the flat roof above. At the far corner of this stood a tiny summerhouse, half buried in the pink leaves of a bougainvillaea vine. To it another little flight of steps led up. There Aunt Anastasia sat beside a low table heaped with muslin. The sunlight, sifting through the vine, flashed on the needle that shot in and out, in and out, between the sprays of rosebuds in her work. Lucita brought a little chair to sit beside her.

"Well, aunty," she said.

Aunt Anastasia paused to smile into the brown eyes now so nearly on a level with hers. Hers were brown, too, and so was the hair that crowned her pretty head. Indeed, people said Lucita resembled her aunt more than she did her stately father, and far more than she did her mother, who had blue eyes and hair like gold.

"How do you like this, *carita?*" inquired Aunt Stasia, holding up a little lace-edged puff.

"Like it?" Lucita's fingers fairly caressed the sprigs of flowers. "Oh, aunty, is it for me?"

Aunt Stasia's smile broke into a laugh of pure pleasure. "Of course it is, dear child. Why, what did you expect to wear to Pancha's party, you poor little ragamuffin?"

Lucita's eyes fell to the gingham frock she had on. A three-cornered tear, reminder of the Tree of the Angels' Hair, certainly did not improve its appearance.

"I—I guess," said she slowly, "I expected the saints to provide."

"Am I one of the saints, then? At any rate, I am almost ready for you to try the dress on; and meantime I want you to be thinking what you would like to have me tell you about to-day."

"*'How do you like this?' inquired Aunt Stasia*"

"I don't have to think," cried Lucita. "Ever since the night of the storm I've waited to ask you about Doña Marina of the Fountain—her story, I mean."

Aunt Anastasia's face grew thoughtful. She looked up from her work to the cathedral opposite, built by Cortés; to his palace, closing the vista of the narrow street; to the vivid green of sugar fields midway between the shimmering valley and the snow-capped peaks of the volcanoes—sugar fields that he had planted three hundred years before. It was a story of the *Conquistador* Lucita asked for, of the Spanish soldier Cortés, who had conquered Mexico, and afterwards received from his emperor twelve cities to rule over, of which Rosario was one.

"Look, Lucita!" she said. "From here you can see the cathedral and the palace and the sugar plantation of Cortés, almost in a straight line. You remember I have told you how he built them, all three? The story of Doña Marina and of Cortés are the same, and this is the way it begins.

"Once upon a time, far, far to the south, but still in Mexico, there lived in a palace a little Indian princess called Malinche. All her life, until she was six or seven years old, she had been kindly treated. She had been taught, too, how to speak in low, sweet tones, how to walk gracefully, how to embroider with the pretty feathers of birds, and, above all, how to worship and obey the gods. Of these gods there were several in her city, each in a high temple of stone shaped like a great pyramid. Some were terrible monsters, to whom sacrifices must be made; but one was gentle and lovely to look upon, Quetzalcoatl, God of the Air. Often in the morning when the dawn winds began to stir in the east, and the humming-birds flitted in and out like rainbows among the brilliant garden flowers, Malinche could almost imagine she saw him returning, as he had promised, to his people. For Quetzalcoatl, so the priests and her mother told her, no longer lived in their land. Long, long ago, in sorrow and in anger, he had sailed away in his magic boat, because his people would not heed him, nor give up their wicked ways. But he had left them a promise: out from the east to which he had gone he would return again. Him Malinche worshiped in her gentle heart, and him she tried to serve.

"In her quiet, pleasant home she was happy, much as my Lucita is. Then, suddenly, one day the prince her father died, and just as suddenly, it seemed to her, a baby prince was born. I think she must have been pleased when they told her about her baby brother, for the palace was very lonely after her father went away, and perhaps, like my Lucita, she had always wanted a playmate. Her mother was pleased also, but she took a very strange way to show it. As soon as she was sure the little boy would live and grow, she took Malinche and sold her to some wandering merchants who happened to be passing through her city. Why? Because she wanted the province she ruled to go to her son, and if Malinche lived he might have to share it with her. Then she told every one that her daughter was dead; yes, and she made a great funeral for her and mourned for her many days.

"If she could but have seen poor little Malinche, borne off by the merchants through the thick jungles and across the broad rivers, perhaps her hard heart might have mourned indeed. Day after day the merchants traveled eastward, halting at this city or at that to sell their wares. In those days there were no roads and no horses in Mexico, so that their

THE LADY OF THE FOUNTAIN

progress was very slow. At length they came to a certain city which was the capital of a powerful prince. Here in the market place they set up their booths. In one of these sat Malinche, dressed in a royal robe of feather work and crowned with a chaplet of gold. They offered her for sale. And the prince, who attended the fair, saw her and was pleased with her, and bought her for himself. So Malinche once more lived in a palace, but no longer as a princess. Even the speech of her master was unknown to her, and she could not understand what she was asked to do. But gradually she learned the new language, and so grew up in attendance on one of the ladies of her master's court.

"From time to time there came to this court strange rumors of great ships seen off the coast. Occasionally chance voyagers wandered into the interior, and it was told by one to another that the strangers were white, like to the gods. At last, on a day, one of these ships dropped anchor at the mouth of the river on which Malinche's city was built. All the warriors, and the prince himself, went down to see what manner of men these were, and what they wanted there. They found the strangers seemingly very friendly. Though they could not understand their words, they exchanged presents with them—girdles and headdresses and golden dishes and rings. In return they received trinkets of bright glass or nickel or tin—wonderful things in their eyes, such as they had never seen. Some of these gifts, with an account of the strangers, the prince dispatched by swift runners to his emperor. You see, in spite of the difference in language, the same emperor ruled over the state where Malinche was born and this distant province of Yucatan. Meantime the Spaniards (for such the strangers really were) sailed back to the island of Cuba and told its governor what a wealthy and gentle people they had visited, and how easily their country could be conquered and added to the Spanish crown; how easily, too, a Spanish knight might enrich himself with the spoil of such simple folk.

"Malinche and her prince, of course, did not know this. They wondered in their hearts if these men, so fair and tall, were not the forerunners of their god's return. They asked the Emperor Montezuma in their letters, and had not long to wait for his reply. Over the mountains, down the valleys, across the marshy plains, the runners bore his answer: 'Gods or men, do not dally with the strangers; if they return, fight.'

"Not many months later they did return, they and others with them; notably a leader so powerful and so fair to look upon that he might well be the god Quetzalcoatl himself. Hundreds followed his standard, tall and fair like him. In the marshes about his city the prince fell on them. Crowded ranks of his best warriors discharged arrows swift as hail. They were answered by blasts of thunder, and lightning that killed where it struck. Clouds of smoke obscured the battle field. Such beings the Indians had never seen. Again they let fly their arrows. But now, behind them, the ground shook with a mighty trampling, and lo! monsters, half man, half animal, swept down upon them, smiting as they passed. At the sight of these terrible beasts the bold warriors wavered and broke and fled. To the forest, to the marshes, to the river they ran to escape from the guns and the horses, the like of which they had never known.

"Afterward the prince sent to the leader, encamped in the city he had lost, tribute of gold and precious stones and slaves. Costly were the presents and beautiful the slaves. Among them was Malinche. She was now about as old as I am, Lucita, and good as she was lovely. The Spaniards saw that she was the fairest of all the captives, and took her to their chief. You guess already who he was, Hernando Cortés, the conqueror of Mexico. Malinche thought as she looked at him that she had never seen any one so beautiful, so like the god of her dreams. From that moment she was ready to serve him. And Cortés, won by her charm, treated her with much kindness, then and afterward.

"In those days he was just starting with his expedition, and he was glad indeed to learn that Malinche knew the languages of both Yucatan and Mexico. From her he found out many things of value about the people among whom he was to go, and in the months that followed she saved him many times. Everywhere that Cortés went, Malinche went with him, treated always with the consideration due her birth, and called by his followers the Lady Marina. They did not have an easy journey from the coast up to Montezuma's capital, the City of Mexico. There were forests to march through, and high, steep mountains to climb. Worst of all, there were Indians everywhere, and everywhere hostile to them, in obedience to the emperor's commands. He did not want the Spaniards marching through his country, and yet he feared them. In the old books of the priests it had been written, long ago, that one day the God of the Air would return. And now the people, looking on the white skin and blue eyes of Cortés, said, like Malinche, 'Is not this the God of the Air, whom the winds and the thunders obey?' So the people wondered, and Montezuma also wondered, and trembled on his throne.

"What Malinche thought when Cortés showed her that he was only a man, after all, we shall never know, except that she still loved and believed in her conqueror with all her simple heart. She helped him to win over the princes along the way until at length they crossed the last mountain barrier and marched down into the Valley of Mexico. The same volcanoes, white-coned Popocatepetl and rugged Ixtaccihuatl, stood sentinel above it. The slopes of the lesser mountains, now so bare, were covered with green forests, and where sandy fields of *maguey* now stretch, the waters of three great lakes danced and rippled in the morning light. On the farther shore rose the massed outline of a noble city: houses surrounded by tropical gardens, canals gay with boats, temples that reared themselves in lofty pyramids to the sun. Here in the palace Montezuma received his unwelcome visitor, and here Malinche told her emperor of the power of the conqueror, and counseled that he yield to his demands. It would have been better for Montezuma had he not done so. That he did, cost him his life and his empire. Cortés laid in ruins his fair city, and with the fall of the city became ruler in his stead. From all over the empire came the subjects of Montezuma, hastening with treasure of gold and silver and precious stones

THE LADY OF THE FOUNTAIN 25

to turn aside the wrath of Cortés, and to swear allegiance to his sovereign, the Emperor of Spain.

"It was in the hour of Cortés's triumph that Malinche came to be loved most by friends and foes alike. Time and again she pleaded for mercy toward her poor countrymen. Her peaceful measures brought to the Spaniards those peaceful victories which are far more lasting than the victories of war. Among both Indians and Spaniards her name was blessed.

"It happened, not long after the conquest of Mexico itself, that Cortés visited the province where Malinche was born. The princess of that country came at once with great pomp and rich presents to treat with him. But when she recognized her daughter, standing on the dais beside him, her heart sank in despair. 'Surely,' she thought, 'they will both kill me, for my wickedness which I have done.' But Malinche in the same instant recognized her mother, and ran to her, and took off her own rings and her necklaces and her brooches and put them upon her, so eager was she to show her mother that she forgave her and loved her and wanted her love in return. Then the poor mother could not doubt her, but rejoiced greatly in the goodness of the gods.

"There, in the land of her fathers, Malinche's wanderings came to an end. There Cortés left her, rich in the estates he gave her, happy perhaps to be reunited to her family and honored by her people. Yet she must have longed often to be with him, especially in the after years when he settled here in Rosario, and went no more to war. They say her spirit came to him in the palace, and in the granary, where he counted over the ingots yielded to him by mines and sugar fields, and especially here by the fountain he built. On moonlight evenings, as he paced back and forth, back and forth, a shadowy lady rose from the depths of the water, rose, and wrung her hands, and disappeared. It was the Princess Malinche. She comes to look for him still."

IV

FRANCISCA'S DAY

THE birthday of Lucita's playmate, Francisca, or Pancha as she was always called, happened to fall on a Sunday this year. But that made no difference in her mother's plans for the party. Indeed, it made more of a *fiesta* of the occasion than usual. For a birthday in Lucita's country is always a saint's day as well. Pancha was born on the day of Saint Francis, as Lucita was on that of Our Lady of Light. There are very many saints in Mexico, enough to go around among all the babies, boys and girls alike.

On the morning of Pancha's birthday mamma slipped very early into Lucita's room. It was light, for the winter sun rises earlier in that southern land than with us. But the bells of the cathedral had not yet rung for mass, and Lucita was still asleep. Her mother tiptoed softly about, opened the shutters, took from their drawers some fresh, dainty underwear, and laid out on the foot of the bed the new sprigged muslin that Aunt Anastasia had made. With the first stroke of the bells Lucita's eyes opened and fell on it.

"Oh, mamma," she cried, "isn't it pretty! And are you going with me to the church?" For she had noticed also her mother's white embroidered gown and the white lace *mantilla* she always wore over her head when she went to mass.

"Yes, dearie, if you please," smiled her mother.

"If I please! Of course I do. I am more pleased to have you than any one else in all the world, my beautiful mamma." And at that Doña María was hugged and kissed and "rumpled"—as Lucita called it—to her heart's content. But if her dress and her hair suffered, her temper did not. I think she enjoyed it.

A half-hour later a very dainty little girl, with each curl as much in place as such unruly curls could be, and each step as sedate as such a happy heart would allow, walked beside her mother across the cathedral square and through the high doorway of the church. The organ was playing, and already the people were kneeling in silent prayer before the high altar. Far up the aisle Lucita spied Pancha and Carmen, side by side. But it was not until after the service —a very long service it seemed that day—that she could speak to Pancha, to wish her a "Happy Birthday."

And it was a much longer time until the cool shadows of the afternoon came, and with them, the hour of Pancha's party. But at last mamma and Tia Stasia had again tied Lucita's pink ribbons and pinned her pink sash. With a farewell kiss to each, she tripped up the street. Even the street seemed trimmed in pink for the day; on either side oleanders and crêpe myrtles cast a fragrant shade. From the fountains servants were bringing buckets of cool water to sprinkle the hot pavements, and through the open gateways as she passed Lucita caught glimpses of fathers and mothers and children sitting out in their cool *patios*. Into one of the gateways, larger and finer than the rest, she turned at length. Here the *patio* was protected from rain by a canopy of glass; bright-colored portulacas and close pruned roses grew in trim beds along the gravel walk, and in the exact center a fountain plashed into a pool where many goldfishes played. All this, Lucita knew, cost money. Pancha's father was a banker, and "as rich as he could be." But, somehow, Lucita felt very much out of place here, "as if," she told mamma afterward, "a wild flower had gotten into a garden."

Nor did she feel more comfortable when the butler brought her to the door of the drawing room and left her there. The drawing room stretched a very, very long distance over its flagged length to the place where Pancha sat. And on either side the walls were lined with chairs, and in each chair sat somebody, nearly always a grown-up, talking and laughing and making a great noise. To be sure, they were only Pancha's uncles and aunts and cousins, and most of them Lucita knew, and, yes, here was one of them coming toward her now, with a pleasant smile on his face. It was none other than Pancha's father himself!

He stooped and kissed her, "for her papa's sake," and patted her hand, and led her to Pancha's side. Carmen was there, too, and Dick and Pablo, and Pancha's father beamed upon them all, and Pancha's mother passed around a basket of sweets, and altogether the party began to be quite a happy affair. And of course Pancha was pleased with the basket of dishes which Carmen had insisted that Lucita must present, after all, and unpacked them immediately, and compared them, and showed them to every one. Then there were other presents to be looked at; a little blue silk *mantilla* that was very lovely indeed on top of Pancha's brown hair, a wonderful Paris doll "that papa brought me and mamma dressed," Pancha confided; handkerchiefs and books and ribbons, and dozens of the things all little girls always have on their birthdays, wherever they live.

"But do you know what we are going to do that will be the most fun of all?" whispered Pancha.

Lucita and Carmen echoed an excited "What?" Even Dick and Pablo became interested.

"We are all going to the park for supper, going to take it in our baskets, and eat it under the trees!"

"Hurrah!" cried Dick.

"But," asked the more cautious Pablo, "will they let us play in our Sunday clothes?"

His father overheard, and laughed. "They will," he said. "On Pancha's day they will let you do as you please. Pancha is queen to-day."

By this time the butler came bustling in again to announce the carriages. All was happy confusion once more, as cousins and aunts and uncles crowded into landaus, and servants and more servants kept running with baskets and bottles, to tuck in under their feet. For a moment it looked as if the children, and even the little queen of the occasion, were going to be forgotten at home. But no, when all the carriages were full, and the last one had rattled away, a troop of donkeys, each with a little seat on its back, came filing into the court. Lucita

"*A merry cavalcade they made, riding down the street*" Page 31

—they said because she was half *Americana*—needed no help to mount; the others were gallantly handed up by Pablo and Dick. A merry cavalcade they made, riding down the street, followed by Alejandro, who kept each lagging donkey up to his proper speed.

"We shall take the short cut," announced Pancha.

"And beat the grown-ups!" cried Pablo.

That last was easily done. Down the steep sides of a ravine, over a ford, and up again, scrambled the hardy donkeys. Fully ten minutes before the carriages arrived the children were sitting, flushed but satisfied, on the wide, curved benches that stood at the entrance to the park. Satisfied, did I say? Not for long.

"Let's go wading," suggested Dick. "What do you say, Queen Pancha?"

Pancha laughed merrily. "Let's."

No sooner said than off came brown shoes and white shoes and black shoes. Stockings followed suit. With pretty skirts and white trousers tucked up, and little screams at the sudden chill of the water, five pairs of feet paddled down the sluiceways that lined the garden paths. Now they came to a tiny cascade, which they had to walk around, and farther on to the pool of a fountain, and at last to a low, rustic bridge. Here they sat on the edge and dangled their feet, and waited for their elders.

"Sh! I hear them coming," they whispered.

Coming they certainly were, down the broad steps, through the promenade beneath the plane trees, out into the square of the fountain, and on to the bridge. More than that, they knew the mischief the children had been in. Five pairs of shoes and stockings hung from hands already full of picnic baskets and parcels. Yet they did not seem to mind, not even when Pancha's mother caught sight of the grass stains on her pretty dress, or felt the damp skirts that heedless little Lucita had forgotten to hold up. Napkins did the duty of towels, and the damage, as far as possible, was repaired.

Then all, grown-ups and children, sat down on the benches to eat the good things they had brought: chicken salads, corn *tortillas*, a cake with nine candles—for all the world like the one Lucita's mother had made for her last year—and, last but not least, orange *nieve* from the ice-cream man, who had been told beforehand to bring it to the grove. By the time they came to this, a group of curious Indian children had begun to gather on the outskirts. Alejandro was among them. Pancha's mother spoke to her in a low voice, and Pancha waved her hand for them to come nearer.

"*A group of curious Indian children*"

"Come," she said. "Come and have ice cream and cake with me."

FRANCISCA'S DAY

You may be sure they went; and the little cups were heaped high for each Indian boy and girl. They ate in silent rapture, and then, with a shy little *"Gracias, niña,"* from Alejandro, they retreated and went on with their own games.

The shadows in the grove had grown very long and cool when the feast was ended. More soberly than they had come, the children rode homeward.

Lucita lingered a moment beside Pancha's mother to say good-by. "I have had such a good time," she said.

"And so has Pancha," said her mother, "and she wants each little girl and boy to take home something to remember her by." In Lucita's hand she placed a tiny book, gayly colored, that bore on it in large capitals the title: "The Story of Malinche." To Carmen she gave another exactly like it. "And tell Doña María," she continued to Lucita, "that we all thank her for Pancha's birthday cake."

"Mamma," cried Lucita a few minutes later, as she ran into her mother's room, "see what Pancha has given me!" She held up the book. "It's the very story Tia Stasia told me last week, the story of our fountain."

Mother held out her arms. "Come, and tell me all about everything," she smiled.

Lucita settled herself very cozily in mother's lap to do so.

"But, *mama mia*," she concluded, *"why* did you make Pancha a cake?"

"Because all-Mexican little girls don't have cakes," she said, "and I thought Pancha would like it, and my Lucita, too."

"We did," Lucita answered, "oh, very much."

V

THE EASTER BIRDS

THE weeks that followed Pancha's party were busy ones for all who belonged to Doña María's household. The Easter holidays were fast approaching and the streets of Rosario began to be crowded by the Americans and English who came here to escape the noisy celebrations in the City of Mexico. Mexicans and Indians likewise flocked in from *haciendas* and outlying hamlets with the entirely opposite idea of seeing the sights. The Plaza and the market took on an air of unusual gayety; boys with toys arranged like huge bouquets of flowers cried their wares at every corner; sellers of ice cream and fruits and sweets set up stands along the sidewalks for the holidays, and opposite the cathedral a new market blossomed in booths where all the knickknacks of the larger market were offered for sale. Across the streets wires were strung at intervals, and from these hung life-size and very ugly images of Judas, made of paper, to be set off, like huge firecrackers, on Easter Day.

At Doña María's also special preparations were being made to catch the Easter trade. It was the first time Lucita fully realized the change of fortune that had overtaken them. In former years, at the capital, their home had been a meeting place for congenial people of many nationalities.

At this season it had overflowed with hospitality and good cheer. Now she saw her mother busy as of old in putting her house in order; yet the difference even Lucita could feel. One day mamma and Aunt Stasia were engaged all day in unpacking boxes that came from the Canary Islands. In them were laces, fine as cobwebs, embroidered gowns, drawn-work table covers and scarfs and mats. Another day the muleteer and Alejandro carried in cases of precious Talavera ware; jars almost as tall as Lucita herself, patterned in blue peacocks and peony flowers; smaller vases, teapots, pitchers, cups and saucers—shelves on shelves to be arranged anew. In the midst of this confusion arrived a drove of donkeys bearing in panniers yet other pottery, that of the Indian village of San Cristóbal on the hill. This was a red ware, much coarser, made into braziers, cooking crocks, and vases, little and big. These were hardly in place before Don Enrique, papa's old partner, stepped off the tram car at the door.

His arrival, though, was made the occasion of a little *fiesta*, for he brought news of papa. Lucita ran to tell Petra to heat the water for tea, and to set the table in the cool arcade. There they gathered, mamma, Aunt Stasia, and Don Enrique, all talking merrily. While

"Boys with toys arranged like huge bouquets of flowers cried their wares at every corner"

they talked and sipped their tea Lucita sat on the floor and played with a bag of opals Don Enrique had brought. For Don Enrique came from papa's old home in the south, a place Don Hilario had not visited in years, a place that no one had thought to take away from him, because no one coveted it. Here, away up in the mountains, Don Enrique had uncovered an opal vein. Some of the stones he brought were large as marbles, and others as small—as small as Lucita's least little pink finger nail. Some flamed like golden drops of fire; others had hearts of violet, and others flashed with sudden lights of green and blue and red, like rainbows. Lucita caught them in her hands and let them fall; she sorted them by colors and by sizes, and picked out "her very own."

All of a sudden her attention was caught by something Don Enrique was saying:

"Yes, I believe this new mine is going to restore our fortunes, and I have written to Hilario to come back. This stone, for instance," and he picked up the largest of Lucita's marbles, a wonderful, fiery pink, "is only a sample of the kind we are getting now. And you know they are the rarest and best of our opals."

Doña María took the stone absently. "When did you write?" she asked.

"About a month ago."

"Then that explains Hilario's last letter to me. He said business was picking up, and he might have a surprise for me soon."

Of course Lucita knew that Hilario was none other than her papa.

"Oh, is papa coming?" she cried. "Is papa coming home to us?" The opals scattered unheeded as she ran to Don Enrique's side.

He put a gentle hand on her curls. "And have you missed him so much, *pobrecita?*" he asked. "Yes; I think papa can come home."

He seated her on his knee and began to talk again with mamma. There were many long sentences in which "the government" was mentioned, and "the estates" and "lawyers" and the "business in New York." But through it all and over it all, like a song, ran the refrain in Lucita's heart, "Papa is coming home!"

After that it was not so hard for even Lucita's impatient little fingers to wait on the customers who came daily in increasing numbers to Doña María's store. Indeed, she was proud to be thought old enough for the responsibility. The trays of opals were put in her special charge. Each one, like her pet sparrows, she knew by name; but as one after another vanished she could not stop to miss them. Every silver dollar meant that papa was drawing nearer, that he was coming home. Lucita had never known the value of dollars before!

Palm Sunday came and went; the people thronged the cathedral, each carrying a palm branch and a flower-wreathed water jar. In happy procession they poured out again, waving the green branches, and carrying more carefully than before the holy water the bishop himself had blessed. Through the streets at night came always the sound of music, for in the Plaza the band played every night. Occasionally, from the theater, floated strains of another band, gradually growing louder as it approached. First marched boys with flaring torches, lighting up a huge sign—the playbill of the evening. The musicians straggled along behind, and the people came out to doorways or balconies to see what the play was going to be. Even Lucita, unable to sleep for the noise, was allowed to sit with the family on the cool roof those nights. Only the bells of the cathedral were silent during the latter part of Holy Week. They were in mourning for the Crucifixion, and in their place wooden clappers called the hours of prayer.

At last the gray light of Easter morning broke over the hills. It was a morning when every one in Rosario arose betimes. There were early mass and high mass to be celebrated, and afterward the images of Judas to be fired off. Doña María and Aunt Anastasia and Lucita went with the rest to church. The high altar glittered with gold and candles; the people, men in spotless white and women in pretty gowns and gay-colored shawls, filled all the space from doors to altar. Before the altar the bishop, in robes of white and gold brocade, sang the mass. Other priests, in gorgeous dress, assisted. Now and again the choir broke into song. Suddenly, in the midst of the Te Deum, the black curtains that had veiled the figures of Christ and the Saints all the week were drawn away. From a recess behind the glory a flock of singing birds flew up to the high-arched roof. The hush that followed was filled with their wild songs. Then every one turned to his neighbor. "Christ is risen," he said.

The service was over, the bells pealed forth, the people, most of them, flocked to the hangings of Judas in the streets. But Lucita and her aunt and her mother went happily and quietly home. "Christ is risen," sang Lucita's heart, "and papa is coming home."

VI

THE COMING OF PAPA

YOU would like Lucita's papa. In the first place, he looked like Lucita, or, as mamma would say, Lucita looked like him. He had brown curls too, and brown eyes, and a mouth that turned up at the corners. And he stood very straight and tall, and looked you straight in the eyes. If you had asked Lucita what papa did, she would have answered that he rode about on trains and on horseback a very great deal, but that, when he was home, he told the most wonderful stories of the places he had seen, and played like some nice, big boy. The stories were all about mines,— silver mines, gold mines, and mines of precious stones. Sometimes he brought the sparkling crystals home to show her, and explained how they were dug out of the dark tunnels in the earth. Sometimes he told her how the Indians, centuries before, worked in these same mines, and how, along the road from Trinidad to Rosario, and from Rosario to the coast, the Spaniards later sent trains of pack mules, carrying the treasure to load on to ships for Spain. Often and often these treasure ships were sunk in some sudden storm, or the pirates who sailed those seas fell upon them and looted and sank them with all on board. But the pirates, in their walled cities, made merry with the spoil.

Now Lucita's father was called a mining engineer; and

that means a man who finds the hiding place of gold and silver and precious stones in the rocky mountain's side, and then finds the best way to dig them out and make them fit for use. This had kept him very busy, for Mexico has many, many mines. Besides, he had mines of his own, handed down in his family for hundreds of years, from the time when the Spaniards conquered the land. But a year ago it suddenly began to be questioned whether he really did own some of his richest mines. Lucita's mother said it was because some one was envious and wanted them himself. And nobody seemed to understand very much more about it than Lucita; only it meant that papa went away to the States, and mamma came to Rosario to open a store.

Lucita was thinking all this over as she sat in the arcade, an arithmetic open before her, and a slate on her knees. She did not like arithmetic, but only yesterday Alejandro had beaten her at the multiplication table, and he an Indian. That must not happen again.

"Eleven times one are eleven, eleven times two are twenty-two," she recited in a kind of singsong that kept pace with the song Chiquito was singing in the cage above her head, "eleven times three—"

"Lucita! Lucita!" It was mamma who called.

Lucita ran in answer, down the arcade, into the hall—and there she stopped. A tall gentleman whose face she could not see was standing with one arm about mamma, and another about Aunt Stasia, until he caught sight of Lucita. Then both arms were held out to her.

With a sharp little cry, "It is papa!" she was gathered into Don Hilario's arms, and kissed, and lifted to his shoulder, and, in short, treated just as if he had not forgotten her for one little minute in all the time he had been away. Meantime mamma cried until she laughed, and Aunt Stasia flitted about, directing Alejandro where to put papa's bags, and whispering to Petra about the marketing, and shutting the doors of the shop. For papa, after all, was a surprise. Now that he was here Aunt Stasia was going to see to it that he was made comfortable. Assuredly, no shop would be kept this day.

Afterward, while papa and mamma were talking together in their room, Lucita went into the garden to pick what flowers there were, in honor of the occasion; great purple pansies, white jasmines, and fragrant honeysuckles. To the flowers she told her happiness.

"I'm picking you," she said to the whitest jasmine of all, "for papa's buttonhole. He has come all the way from New York, in the United States of America. And he's not going away any more. He has brought presents, too. I don't know what yet; I haven't asked him. But do you s'pose—" she paused at a sudden idea—"do you s'pose he thought to bring me my little brother?"

With that, the last flower was hastily dropped into the basket, and Lucita ran back to the house.

Standing close beside papa, she reached up and pinned the flower in his coat. And then she pulled him down to whisper into his ear—something that made papa look at mamma and laugh.

"What is it, Hilario?" asked mamma.

"Our Lucita has just asked me," papa answered as he kissed Lucita's pretty curls, "if I brought a little brother for her from New York."

"It is something she has wanted for a long time," said mamma gravely. "Perhaps you will bring him another time. To-day, Lucita, he came in a great hurry. But he has some things in his bag that our little girl will like."

At that moment Aunt Stasia came to say that luncheon was ready. "Except," she amended, "the flowers Lucita didn't bring."

"Oh, aunty, I forgot."

"Never mind, little girl," said papa. "We will arrange them all together. That will be much nicer." And hand in hand they set out for the dining room.

That was a luncheon worth remembering! Turkey and chestnuts and sauces, salads and ice cream. Petra, flushed and beaming, served the courses herself. But, somehow, nobody seemed to have much time to notice what there was to eat. Papa had so many interesting things to say that even Petra forgot her serving in listening to such marvels. He told of the tall buildings which had gone up since mamma had come from New York to marry him; of the subway, and of the crowded downtown offices where he had been busy all the long, long months. These things were far more strange to Lucita's ears than they would be to yours.

After luncheon the bags were brought out, and tne presents spread to view, presents brought from this same wonderful city so far away. There were a pair of shoes and a locket for Petra, a knife for Alejandro, some shimmering silks for mamma and Aunt Stasia, and books and pictures for Lucita. The pictures Lucita could understand, but the books were in

The Hacienda

English. Lucita knew how to read Spanish, but English she could only speak. Papa smiled at her puzzled frown as she turned the pages of "Mother Goose" and "The Adventures of Robin Hood."

"My Lucita will have to take lessons of mamma, as I did," he said. "She is the best of teachers, not excepting aunty here."

"Mamma will have time to teach her," smiled Doña Maria, "now that you have come home."

It was in the plans for that home that the best surprise of all came out. Lucita, in her little white nightgown, was just hopping into bed. On the chair beside her were her new treasures, ready to be looked at at the first peep of day. Mamma was waiting to tuck her in.

THE COMING OF PAPA

"How would you like it, Lucita, to go away from Rosario?"

"With you and papa?" asked Lucita.

"Yes, indeed."

"Where to?"

"To the beautiful country," mamma answered; "to a place where there are no shops, and no streets, and no people; to the place where papa lived when he was little like you."

"I know, I know," cried Lucita, while her eyes danced—and the bed danced too, as she jumped up and down in her joy—"to the Hacienda and the opal mines!"

At the commotion, papa came in.

"So," he said, "she would like it?" And then he and mamma both sat down on the edge of the bed, and told Lucita, and each other, all about their plan, until Lucita's sleepy little head could hold no more. But I am not going to tell you. You shall find it out for yourselves.

VII

SAN ANGEL

DOWN in the hot country, at the foot of a mountain so steep that its cliffs looked like battlemented castles against the sky, lay the Hacienda of San Angel. Other mountains, with slopes more gradual, hemmed it into a spreading valley. Through it ran a clear, tree-shaded stream. On either side, up hill and down, as far as the eye could reach, stretched fields on fields of sugar cane. In the fields men were working, cutting the tall stalks, binding them in great sheaves on the backs of mules, or piling them into carts. Other men with long goads drove the patient oxen to the mill, the smoke from which rose black against the mountain behind. Others, on horseback, escorted the trains of mules; and yet others drove back the empty ricks. Everywhere, along the dusty roads and in the green fields, the white trousers of the workers gleamed in the hot sunlight, like swarms of white and busy bees.

Through the valley ran also a railroad, and on the tracks a train was coming, the train from Rosario. The whistle

Great sheaves of sugar cane were bound to the backs of mules

shrieked, the bell rang, the brakes were put on, and amid a din redoubled by the echoing valley, the engine stopped at the station of San Angel. From one of the cars stepped some friends of ours, papa, tall and helpful, mamma, Aunt Stasia, Lucita, Petra, each carrying bundles or flowers, and last and least, Alejandro, with Chiquito's baize-covered cage. At the curb a stage was waiting, and into it the family climbed. Bareheaded Indians greeted the master and handed up the bundles; the major-domo himself helped to strap on the trunks. Lucita, all eyes, looked curiously at the busy scene. Alejandro, nearly left behind, scrambled over the wheel to a place beside the driver; the whip cracked, and they were off. Up, up, through the cane fields toiled the creaking carriage, with a swaying, rhythmic motion. Overhead, above the shimmering valley, two buzzards circled. Lucita watched them wheeling, now near, now far, now—but Lucita had fallen asleep.

When she woke it was to find herself being carried up some broad stone stairs. At the top was a flagged gallery, vine-shaded and cool, even on this sultry day. Papa, for it was he who held her, took her into a big, square room and laid her on a bed. Then mamma came in and put a soft hand on her hot head. Little Light was very tired. The packing, the crowd of friends at the station, the long, dusty ride in the train, had been too much for her. With a sigh of content she shut her eyes and went to sleep once more.

In her dreams she found herself back in Rosario. Pancha was kissing her good-by and promising to come to see her as soon as she could. Carmen was crying, and Lucita was crying, too. Pablo was the only one of the playmates who offered any comfort. He said he had been talking to Alejandro. Alejandro used to live at the Hacienda before his mother brought him to Rosario. He thought his old home a beautiful place, and he said he was going to be Lucita's special servant there, and he would do all he could so that she should not be too lonesome. All this had really happened, and poor, tired Lucita thought she was living it over again.

It was nearly dusk when she roused, to the sound of a steady crunch, crunch, beneath her window, and a whirring of restless wings. For a moment she lay bewildered, then she ran to the casement. Outside, a light shutter screened her balcony from the western sun. From this balcony she looked down upon the stock yard, where oxen, mules, donkeys, cows, and horses were feeding after their hard day's work. Alejandro, already at home in his old haunts, called up to her.

"See, Lucita, see this baby colt!"

At the too familiar touch of the boy's hands the colt frisked its stubby tail and darted away. A black cloud of ricebirds, scared by the sudden clatter, rose and circled the balcony, and settled down again. The oxen looked up lazily, and then went on with the steady crunching of their dried cornstalks.

So interested was Lucita in her unfamiliar surroundings that she did not hear Aunt Stasia knock, nor know that she was close beside her until she spoke.

"How is our Lucita now? Ready for a little supper?"

Lucita turned a glowing face. "Indeed I am, aunty." Her eyes traveled across the stock yard, across the cane fields, to the brown hills beyond. Not a house was to be seen in all the green acres, on any of the darkening slopes. The first stars came out, and hung low above the silent valley. "Oh," she whispered, "is it not beautiful, and big, and nice to live in!"

Supper was served that night out on the gallery, and the major-domo was host. Not an article on the table, he explained, but had come from the estate. There were broiled chickens "tender as Lucita's heart," omelets smoking hot for each plate, a salad of lettuce and alligator pear, a wonderful rice pudding, fruits of such shapes and flavors as you have never seen, and fragrant chocolate, whipped to a froth. Lucita's father listened as the major-domo gave an account of his year's work. He went to the balustrade and watched the black smoke still pouring from the sugar mill, and the Indians still busy unloading the cane in the courtyard below. For in the sugar season, night and day, day and night, the work goes on. He looked out over the moonlit fields. Then he turned to the major-domo.

"It is good," he said. "And it is good to be at home."

The major-domo, who had waited only for this praise, bowed and clanked away, his spurs striking each stone step in turn.

"It is good," repeated papa to mamma, "but I wish I had a better house to bring you to."

Mamma's eyes followed his to the roof, where the stars

could be seen peeping between the tiles. "But, Hilario," she answered gayly, "what can you expect? You have not been here for ten whole years. And I'm sure it is better than our house in Rosario."

"Is it not?" cried Lucita.

"Well, at least, it can be repaired and made over. And I shall have two, no three, architects to help me." He looked quickly from one to another. "I think in a few years we can have just such a home as we would like."

"I think," said mamma, "it is that now."

At the door of the sugar house

VIII

THE SUGAR MILL

THE next morning, very early, the bells in the mill tower called the hands to work in the fields. They waked little Alejandro, curled up in his father's blanket in the Indian village on the hill. They waked Little Light in her airy room. Down below her window the horses whinnied, and crunched their stalks of grain. Presently the milk began to fall with a hissing noise into the deep, tin pails. Now and then José or Tomas called back and forth, and now and then Pobrecita, the baby colt, whimpered at her mother's heels. Lucita lay and listened in wondering content to the peaceful sounds. Below them all she could hear from the courtyard the steady rumble of the mill.

Long before the breakfast hour she was up and out. Among the strange and busy figures in the yard she spied one that she knew. It was Alejandro. He stood at the door of the sugar house, watching the men at work, his steeple hat, almost as big as he was, pushed back. Lucita ran across to him. At her "Good morning," he turned and slipped his brown hand over her whiter one. From where they stood, Lucita could see, at the far end of the building, a great water wheel turning round and round. Between her and it was a platform. At one end a rick, piled high with cane, was being unloaded and the stalks fed into rollers that crushed out the juice.

This juice ran in a steady stream down a narrow sluiceway, while the flattened stalks were flung into a pile, to be fed to the furnace below.

"Where does the juice go to, Alejandro?" asked Lucita, after she had watched for several minutes the ceaseless task.

"Come, and I will show you," he answered.

Sugar rick

Down the hill, a few feet away, was another house, where in huge vats the sirup boiled and seethed. Men who stood on narrow platforms skimmed it from time to time.

"See," said the boy, "the juice runs first into this vat Down below is a furnace, which heats it very hot. From this, it is strained into this second tank, and from that into this lower one here. Look how clear it has become."

Indeed, it was clear; like liquid amber it was drawn off into huge, brown jars, which were ranged along the walls. They were just the shape of the sugar cones Lucita used to see in Rosario, on the counter of the "Light of Day."

"Oh," she cried, "I see now how they come out that way!"

"Yes," said one of the men, who seemed to be busy plastering over the top of each jar with something moist and sticky. "But that isn't all we have to do to make the white sugar cones you buy. Do you see this?" He pointed to the covers he was putting on. "It is clay, and we seal each of these jars away from the air, and set them in a dark, cool place to bleach the sugar white."

"And that isn't all," added Alejandro. "Wait until you see the roof where the cones are set to dry."

But Lucita was not to see those this morning. In the house across the court a great commotion had arisen. "Where is

A sugar house

Lucita?" papa asked mamma, and mamma asked Aunt Anastasia, and Aunt Anastasia asked Don Enrique, who had just ridden over from the mine. Then, all together, they asked Petra.

Petra, coffeepot in hand, leaned over the high balustrade. "Where is Alejandro?" she demanded of one of the Indians below.

"In the sugar house," returned the man.

"Go and fetch him, and tell him to bring the little mistress with him. I don't know, señorita," she continued to Doña Maria, "that Lucita is with him, but I think so."

"I think so, too," answered Doña Maria, catching sight of Lucita's pink dress as she emerged from the sugar-house door.

Presently she came running up the steps, a ball of clay in one hand, a length of cane in the other, and a very dirty, very happy face above. Even Aunt Stasia, the strictest of her grown-ups, had not the heart to scold her, but took her away and scrubbed her and set her down, still happy, to her bowl of rice and milk.

But as she sprinkled the brown sugar she liked best over her rice, Lucita was struck by a puzzling idea. "Papa," she said, "if all the sugar is bleached, where does the brown sugar come from?"

"What an inquiring little girl we have this morning," said papa, with a smile. "The brown sugar comes from the skimmings, which run into another tank you did not see. It comes, too, from the sirup that oozes out of the jars which have been set away to bleach."

"Is it clean, then?" she asked dubiously.

Don Enrique laughed. "They skim that tank, too; and from those last skimmings is made the cleanest, most sparkling liquor in all the world—alcohol."

"Do we make alcohol, Hilario?" asked mamma, who really knew very little more about a sugar plantation than Lucita.

"Yes," answered papa. "But there is one thing we do not do. We do not sell it to our Indians. The other great landowners do, dear, and the poor Indians spend all their money for it to drink."

With that, he and Don Enrique began to talk earnestly about the evils of this practice, and about many other weighty matters.

But Lucita finished her breakfast, and ran away to put the largest lump of sugar she could find between the bars of Chiquito's cage.

IX

THE CAVE OF WATERS

THOSE first months at the Hacienda were busy ones for Lucita's papa. Often his breakfast was ready with the early bells, and the clatter of his horse's hoofs on the court told that he had set out once more to inspect his huge plantation. Often, too, he went to the mine to consult with Don Enrique, and did not return until night. Usually Alejandro's father rode with him; sometimes he went alone. Not only was the work in the fields and at the mine to be looked over; his mind was busy with plans to put more acres under water, and to better the condition of the Indians so that more would want to settle here and till his lands. His mine was already bringing in money for his use, and every day he became more absorbed in his farming.

As for the water, the major-domo had seen to the building of the tiny canals of masonry that led it from mountain springs miles on miles through the winding valleys. But Don Hilario had heard of a larger spring than any now in use, high up among the mountains, in a deep cave. The noise of it, so the old Indian who told him of it said, was like that of a great river. Don Hilario, who knew that country to be full of caves, unexplored and often very deep, believed that this might be so. And, if so, the cave would be worth more to him than a silver mine in Trinidad, more than his opal mine among the western hills. With such a flood of water at his command, he could see his sugar fields waving like a sea of green to the very threshold of the mountains. Railroads, not trains of mules, should convey the ripened stalks to the mill. And the mill itself, no longer the primitive contrivance of his fathers, but modern throughout, should produce its hundreds of sugar cones a day. In the midst, like a greener oasis, royal palms and evergreen fig trees should shade his courtyard. Fountains were to play there, and grass carpet the bare earth; the old hacienda house, remodeled, should rise in towers and balconies to crown the scene. So Don Hilario dreamed, and the dreams he told to his wife.

Of all this Lucita, though she listened often on papa's knee, took little notice. To her the old house, just as it was, with its cool rooms above and its dark offices below, seemed like a fairy castle. The courtyard, with the constant passing in and out, the garden beyond, the chicken houses on the upper slope, the mango tangle where she and Alejandro played, all these were of never-fading interest. She could imagine no more delightful spot in all the world. Lately, too, her circle of enjoyments had widened.

One day papa called her to the doorway to see a pony that was eating sugar-cane from his hand. It was a little black pony, with two white hind feet, like stockings, and a white, velvety nose. He ate the bits of cane with relish, and hunted around for more. He found them, too, tucked away in one of papa's pockets. Papa laughed at that, and called him a clever little horse.

"Don't you think so, Lucita? How would you like to feed him?"

Of course Lucita did like to, and presently the pony was following her around like a big, pet dog.

"What is his name, papa?" she asked.

"That is for you to say, little daughter. What would you like to call him?"

"What would I like— Oh, papa, do you mean that he is mine?"

"Indeed I do," said papa. "Look here." And from his office he brought a little blanket, and a little saddle, and a bridle of horsehair that just fitted the pony's little head. "Now you shall have your first lesson," and he swung her into her seat.

Was Lucita afraid, do you think? Not a bit of it. Perhaps that was because papa was such a good rider, and his papa, and all the Alarcóns before him. At any rate, she settled happily into her stirrups and laughed up to her mother, who stood looking down from the gallery. That first ride was followed by many others, until José had orders to bring Pajarito or Birdie (as Lucita named him because of his quick, bird-like motions), as regularly as he did the horse his master rode. Sometimes it was Aunt Stasia who went with her, sometimes papa or Don Enrique, and sometimes all four clattered away together, the faithful José holding open the gate, and swinging it shut behind them.

One morning an early shower hardened the roads and freshened the young grass that was making green the brown hill slopes. In the bottom lands the willows were all in tasseled yellow, and around the Indian huts on the opposite hill the cactus hedges had sprung into vivid flower. The dry, winter season was over, and the summer rains had come to

The Indian huts

refresh the thirsty earth. The air, sparkling clear, seemed to magnify the white cones of the volcanoes overtopping the nearer ranges. The family gathered on the gallery to enjoy the perfect day. Even the courtyard was peaceful now, and the sugar mill was closed. The sugar season had ended, and the cones waited only to be loaded on to cars and taken to the city to be sold.

"I think," said papa, "I shall go to explore the cave this morning. Perhaps Stasia and Lucita would like to come, too."

The horses were waiting, and a lunch was quickly prepared. They mounted and rode away. A sharp canter brought them to a narrow trail leading up, up among the mountains. At first it followed the windings of the irrigating ditch which brought the clear water to the fields below. But it was not

THE CAVE OF WATERS 59

long until they passed the reservoir, shimmering like a little lake in a frame of green trees and vines. Farther on they came to an Indian hamlet, perched high on one of the hills. The lane between the huts seemed full of dogs, and pigs, and turkeys scurrying this way and that from under the horses' feet. It took a steady hand to guide the restless ponies through this din and confusion. At the last house in the village they drew up. Here lived the old Indian who had told Don Hilario of the cave. Evidently he was expecting his master, for his horse stood ready saddled, and after a pleasant greeting he headed the procession.

Single file now, up a trail that grew every moment steeper, the ponies climbed. Now they clung to the edge of a precipice, down which one could look hundreds of feet; now they wound their way among trees, where one had to be very careful not to be brushed off by some low branch. At the top of the ridge they paused to rest.

"Are you getting tired, Lucita?" asked papa. "Would you and Tia Stasia like to stay and rest here until I come back?"

It was a pretty place to rest in, under the shade of wild fig trees, beside a bubbling spring.

But Lucita shook her head. "No, indeed; I'm not any more tired than Pajarito—and he isn't tired at all."

Neither was Aunt Anastasia tired. "The very idea of being tired," she exclaimed, "with a real cave to explore!" You can see she wasn't *very* old.

So on they all went, this time down a rocky cañon, and up the opposite side. Now and then a covey of quail started from the bushes, brown and speckled, and piping shrilly as they flew away. Brilliant parrots, in coats of green and red and gold, scolded at them from the tree tops. Once a great lizard, almost as large at Lucita herself, crawled from the path to his hole in the rocks. That, papa explained, was an *iguana;* and the old Indian added that it was very good to eat. But the prettiest sight of all came just as they rounded a cliff which had hidden the trail beyond. There, on the very top of the cañon wall, stood a brown buck! His head was raised to look at them, his wide branching antlers and his tense body outlined like a painting against the blue sky. For a moment he paused, then with a bound he crashed down the slope and out of sight.

"Oh," breathed Lucita, "was he not beautiful?"

"If the señor only had a gun," mourned the Indian.

"But the señor has," said Don Hilario, pointing to his holster. "He did not wish to shoot to-day. I think he felt something as Lucita here did; the picture was too beautiful."

"Alas for the venison steaks, señor, that we might have broiled by the fire!"

"True," answered Don Hilario, "but we will eat ham instead."

Evidently old Pedro was getting hungry, for at the mention of food he put spurs to his horse. At a faster pace the party rode on, until, straight before them, at the end of the cañon, they saw the mouth of the cave. It was huge and dark, but inviting too; for green trees and hanging vines made an arbor about its entrance, and the cool, damp air was very refreshing to the hot and dusty travelers. From Don Hilario's saddle-bags various packages were taken and laid carefully against the rocks; then the saddles were removed and the ponies hobbled. The blankets served as cushions for Lucita and Aunt Stasia to sit on, while papa and Pedro went in search of wood. It was not long before they came back, and Pedro set about making the fire. Nor was it long before the coffee was made, and the ham and eggs fried—and eaten, too, by four very hungry people.

Then papa was ready to explore. In the embers he and Pedro lighted torches of pitch pine. Lucita and Aunt Stasia followed a little way. The flickering light of the torches fell upon walls of wonderful crystal that gleamed like diamonds. Sometimes the crystals hung in clusters from the roof; sometimes they sprang like cathedral arches into the gloom above; they formed pillars and arbors, all of crystal stone. But soon the passage grew narrower and steeper, leading down into the dark. From the blackness below could be heard the sound of rushing waters, very terrible in that wild place.

Lucita was frightened. "Oh, papa," she cried, "you are not going down there!"

"There, there, little girl," papa answered, "of course I am not; but Pedro is, because he knows the way. Don't be frightened. See, I am going to take you and aunty out into the bright sunlight, and very soon I will come back to you there."

Even Aunt Stasia seemed nervous, however. "You won't do anything rash, Hilario?"

"No," he promised. "I took only Pedro because the fewer who know of this the better. He is sure-footed as a cat and has been down before, he says. There are steps cut in the solid rock like a ladder. It is a well his ancestors used, hundreds of years ago."

Whether it were a long time or not, it seemed so to Lucita, while she waited for papa to return. Even Aunt Stasia's stories of the little Indian girls who used to draw water here in the olden time failed to interest her. But when she saw papa actually coming, with a wonderfully happy smile on his face, she forgot her anxiety.

"We have found it!" he cried. "Come, Pedro, bring the jar of water. Lucita, you shall drink first, to the river that is going to make us rich once more." He lifted the brown jug and placed it in her hands. "Drink," he said, "long life to the Hacienda of San Angel!"

X

A LETTER

YOU must not suppose that even Pajarito, or the discovery of a cave, or papa himself, could make Lucita forget her playmates in Rosario. She missed them, and often wished that they could come to see her in San Angel. She missed them so much, indeed, that one day she spoke to Aunt Anastasia about it, and asked her if she would not help her to write a letter to Pancha. Of course Aunt Stasia helped her, and this it what they wrote:

"My dearest friend Pancha," it began, "have you ever seen a mink? I have one, but it is not a pet. It lived by the ditch that brings the water to papa's garden. There, under the bushes, it had a lovely, cool home. Not far away is the chicken yard. Papa lets Alejandro and me help take care of the chickens. They are hatching out of their shells now every day; white ones and yellow ones, and brown ones—such fluffy little balls.

"Well, yesterday morning early Alejandro called me and told me to come quick, because something had caught my very prettiest chicken of all. I ran, but by the time I got there it and the chicken had both disappeared. Alejandro said it was a mink which had done it. I cried, I guess. Alejandro didn't; he knew where that mink lived, and he climbed up there, and he made a trap. It looked like a long, open box, and fastened in it was a kind of noose of wire, and fastened to that, a bit of raw meat. He left it there all night; and this morning—what do you think? Down in the water was the box, turned over, and the mink inside! He wasn't drowned, either, for we could hear him gnawing a hole to get out. If it hadn't been for papa I think he would have, and run way to eat our chickens again. But papa slid some wire netting under the box, and lifted little Mr. Mink right out. He is in a cage now, a wire cage that Alejandro's father made for him. He could, you see, because he is the blacksmith. He is very cunning (the mink, I mean), all brown and yellow and furry, with such bright eyes. But I don't think he can be very happy, do you?

"The name of my horse is Pajarito. He is ever so much more fun than a donkey; he takes me riding every day. Sometimes papa comes, too, and sometimes Aunt Stasia. Last month we were gone all day, and explored a cave. But papa explained that I must not say very much about that, so I will tell you of a visit to the potters of Las Palmillas instead. Of course there are potters right near Rosario, but I don't think you ever went to see them, did you? I didn't, I know, and I never saw how the pots and jars we could buy in the market were made. Here we have no market, except sometimes a very tiny one in the Indian village, when some peddlers pass through. But we have to have dishes, and especially in the sugar season we have to have molds for the cones. So when we want such things we go to the potters for them. They live, a whole village of them, up beside the clay banks on the

A LETTER

mountain. We have to ride, or walk, because there is no road.

"It was an earthquake that made us have to hurry to the potters this week. I suppose you felt it, too. Here, it rocked the house so that almost every one of the jars hanging in the kitchen fell off the nails and broke on the floor. It broke some of the tiles, too, and they came rattling down. It was terrible. We were all very much frightened, and poor Chiquito—you remember Chiquito—didn't sing for a whole day afterward.

"Vicente was the potter we went to see, Aunt Stasia and I. He has a little girl about as old as I am. She is called Dolores. While Aunt Stasia was looking over the things she wanted Dolores took me to the yard, where her mother was making a dish. She took a handful of clay first from a great, big jar.

"Vicente was the potter we went to see"

Dolores told me this clay had been dug from the bank behind the house, and sifted very fine, and wet, and put away in the jar for a long time. Dolores sprinkled a little, flat table with dry earth, and her mother laid the clay on it and kneaded it just the way Petra kneads bread. All of a sudden she took it off, and set it in the center of a round kind of wheel. She turned this so fast that I couldn't see just what she did, except to pat it here and there. And then she stuck sticks into it, all the time twirling it and brushing away what looked like shavings of clay. When the wheel stopped, there stood a jar, just like those you buy, only wet and dark.

"Dolores and I took the jar then and set it in the sun. She says it has to stay so until it is all dry. Then they wash it in what they call a glaze; and her father makes a big fire in the courtyard that burns until only hot ashes are left. Into these he puts all the dishes they have made, and covers them with straw, and heaps earth on top, and leaves them until they are baked. When they are taken out, Dolores says, they are ready to use.

In the potters' village

"I like Dolores. I asked her to come and play with me sometimes. But she said she was too busy. She said if I would come to see her she would teach me how to be a potter. How would you like to have some dishes I made? It seems queer to me that Dolores doesn't make more dishes for herself. I looked in the house where they live. It is built of reeds, and has a thatch roof and only one room, like all the Indian houses. The floor is of earth, and the beds are just mats. In one corner was a place for a fire, and around it stood four or five jars. That was all they had. Do you suppose they like to live that way? Papa says they do.

"I wish you could come for a visit. I can beat Alejandro at

arithmetic, but he can pick more mangoes than I. We have a mango grove. We would play there. And we would go to see Dolores.

A potter of Las Palmillas

"Now I will tell you a secret. Before long I am going to have some one to play with, some one my very own. They've promised him to me for a New Year's present. You can't guess what—a little brother!

"I would like to send my respects to your papa and mamma. To you, Panchita, I send my love.

"Your little *amiga*,
"Lucita de Alarcón.

"P.S. Chiquito sings more than he did in Rosario. His cage is hung among the vines in the gallery. One day a big lizard tried to eat him. They climb up the wall sometimes But Chiquito knows we will take care of him, and he is happy all day long.

"P.P.S. How is Carmen, and how do you like to go to school?"

XI

THE RAID

THE autumn days, clear, bright, and rainless, succeeded the showery summer before an answer came to Lucita's letter. Then, one noon, it stepped off the train in the shape of Pancha herself. And this is how it happened.

Pancha had an uncle who lived down near the Hacienda of San Angel, a *jefe politico*. A *jefe politico* is a very important person, a kind of sheriff and judge all in one. There had been trouble on Don Hilario's place, trouble on account of the cave. Up in the mountains lived a tribe of Indians who had never worked for Don Hilario, nor for any one else. Like the Indians of our own West, this village laid claim to all the lands wrested by the Spaniards from it, centuries before. At that time, they said, they had lived in a well-built city on the plains below, and water carried by stone aqueducts from this same cave had supplied them and their fields of growing maize. It was their cave, the secret of which had been discovered by Don Hilario through what they called the treachery of old Pedro.

All this had been told to Don Hilario by a deputation of about twenty men, who came riding into the court one morning like a whirlwind. Each man had a long knife thrust into his belt, and as they mounted up the stairway, with soft, noiseless steps, they filled Lucita's heart with a nameless dread. What were they going to do with papa? But papa rose to meet them, and stood very stiff and straight until they had said what they wanted. Not even money could buy their water, they told him; it was theirs, and they would defend it with their lives. Then, as noiselessly as they had come, they went, jumped on their horses, and were gone.

Of course this meant nothing else than war—a little war, but a bitter one all the same. Don Hilario's bananas and mangoes began to disappear; now and then one of his workers, straying too far

Making tortillas

from his companions, was found wounded or dead. The hands were in a state of terror. Don Hilario sent to the *jefe* for authority to punish the outlaws. The *jefe* replied by coming in person with a troop of soldiers. At the same time he brought his wife and Pancha, who had been staying with them, "to be company for the ladies during the campaign." The *jefe* laughed as he said this, and Doña Maria could not help smiling in reply. Surely, if he trusted them there, the trouble could not be serious. She thanked him very graciously, and kissed his wife, Doña Felicia, and showed her to her room.

As for Lucita, she was happiness itself. All the long weeks of anxiety were forgotten. Out in the courtyard the soldiers were already being served with *tortillas* and *aguardiente*, and a band of Indians, under the direction of the major-domo, was clearing the sugar houses to serve as barracks. Surely nothing could withstand such brave looking troopers! And was it not fun to think that they had come to protect her castle? It was like an adventure from the pages of Robin Hood!

These thoughts she communicated to Pancha while she took her around to show her her treasures; first, her room with its extra cot all white and waiting, then the chicken yard and the shady mango grove, and last, but by no means least, Pajarito, who obligingly ate sugar from Pancha's hand. Alejandro, too, had to be summoned, and he dug his bare toes into the dust, and swung off his big hat by way of welcome, and then suddenly climbed up into a fig tree and brought them each a handful of the ripe, black fruit.

As they turned back to the house Lucita said, "I am going to take you up to the roof now, where it is nice and cool."

This flat roof above the offices, where in the sugar season the cones were set to dry, made an airy afternoon retreat. There the two girls sat in a hammock, and ate their figs, and talked. Pancha was delighted with the view of fields and mountains; in fact, she was delighted with everything. She told Lucita about Carmen, and about the embroidery lessons they had at the convent. They were making a robe for his Grace, the archbishop, all worked in bunches of white

The two girls sat in a hammock and talked Page 70

THE RAID

violets. Each girl made one bunch. But most of all, she asked questions about the Hacienda. She had never been so far into the country before, and certainly she had never been in such an exciting country as this.

"It's lots better than ghosts and haunted fountains to think what might happen if real bandits attacked you some dark night!" she said with a delicious shiver.

Lucita shivered, too, but she was thinking once more, "What if they hurt papa!"

Just then they heard some one coming, and presently Petra appeared. In her hands she carried a tray, and on it a frosted pitcher of lemonade, and a plate of caraway cookies.

"Why, it is Petra!" cried Pancha. "How do you do?"

"How are you, señorita?" returned Petra with a curtsey, as she set down her tray. "Do you still like cookies as well as you used to in Rosario?"

"Your cookies, at least," said Pancha prettily. "There are none like them there now."

That was a wonderfully short afternoon to Lucita and to Pancha, up on the old, flat roof. All too soon came the call to supper, and bedtime with the dusk.

Much later in the night a stealthy cavalcade issued from the Hacienda gate and took the mountain trail. At its head rode the *jefe* and Don Enrique and Don Hilario; two by two the soldiers followed, their muskets slung across their backs, and pistols in the holsters at their sides. But Lucita did not see them; only Doña María and Doña Felicia watched from the balcony until darkness hid the band. So silently they went that not even the dogs in the village barked as they rode by; so silently that Lucita and Pancha, who had kept each other awake a long time imagining all sorts of terrors, did not stir from their peaceful sleep.

It was not until the next morning that the Hacienda woke to what had happened. At dawn the troop returned, and in their midst walked a band of prisoners. Completely surprised and surrounded, the Indians had surrendered without a shot. To a man they had been taken, and here they were! Don Hilario and Don Enrique and the *jefe* came to breakfast, a little hungrier than usual, perhaps, but otherwise as if nothing had happened. Not so the ladies of the garrison. I think some of them cried, and some of them laughed, and Lucita and mamma, at least, expected to be kissed and petted a good deal. But finally, between the *jefe* and papa, the story of the night's work was told, and everybody reassured. One would have supposed raids on Indian villages were of no more importance than cutting a field of cane, and of no more danger, either.

"Anyway," ended the *jefe* with a flourish, "those Indians will trouble our good Don Hilario no longer."

"But what becomes of them now?" asked Dona Maria, eying uneasily the closely guarded group in the yard.

"I shall take them along with me to Trinidad this afternoon," said the *jefe* crisply. "I need them to work on the road. If we could get a few more villages like this, we should have carriages running to our capital, instead of having to ride over the trail."

"Aren't they going to be tried?" Doña María's American ideas of justice differed from the *jefe's*.

"Tried? Why should I try them, when I have the word of a gentleman like Don Hilario as to what they have done? Surely, my dear lady, you would rather your husband stayed with you than went to Trinidad to accuse these men?"

"Surely I would," said Doña María, and she questioned justice no more.

XII

THE RUINS OF ATLAN

IT was during the *jefe's* absence that papa took the household to the ruins of Atlan. Atlan was the city on the plain, where the Indians said their ancestors had lived. It lay about six miles from the mansion, but still on the estate. The trail was an easy one, so easy that papa undertook to drive mamma and Doña Felicia. The two little girls rode horseback. Alejandro's father was the guide, and Alejandro himself perched behind his father on a very lively little horse. Don Enrique and Aunt Stasia brought up the rear. Besides their luncheon, papa took picks and shovels in the wagon, for they were going to dig in the ruins.

"Papa says," Lucita explained to Pancha, the day before the expedition, "that you can find toys of clay and stone all about; little figures like dolls that used to be idols, and dishes and arrowheads."

"What are arrowheads?" asked Pancha.

"They are what the Indians used to shoot with," answered papa, who had joined them; "triangular pieces of hard stone that they fastened on to wooden shafts, and shot from bows. I will show you some when we get to Atlan; and we shall find knives, too, and needles, and hatchets, all made of stone."

"Am I not part Indian, papa?" asked Lucita.

"Indeed, yes; we all are, and we're proud of it, too. That

is what made the poor Indians up in the mountains so very much in the wrong; for Ruiz de Alarcón, who was given these lands at the time of the conquest, married a princess of the tribe of Atlan."

"Oh," cried Pancha, "I wonder if I am part princess, too, Lucita, like you."

Papa laughed. "I'm afraid not, little Panchita. I think your father is just as proud not to be part Indian as we are to be. He came straight over from Spain."

"But," said Lucita, as she looked at Pancha's disappointed face, "they have lords and ladies over there even yet, Pancha, and not dirty Indians for cousins. Why, I suppose that's why you have gray eyes and light hair, and why I am so dark. Please, doesn't that make you feel better?"

I think it did; anyway, Pancha was as sunny as Lucita on the morning of the picnic, and raced her horse over the level stretches with as light a touch on the rein. Up gentle hillocks and down long hollows they wound, until, in the distance, they could see a square mound topping a hill. All about, the country, brown once more except for the flowers of the cosmos and coreopsis, sloped miles upon miles to the mountains. Like white clouds, the white cones of the volcanoes floated in the eastern sky. They all halted to enjoy the view.

Perhaps an hour later they climbed to the base of the mound. Their horses they had left in a little cañon below. There, beside a pool, was a meadow, still fresh from the summer rains, where they could eat and drink. As Lucita followed her father across the piles of stone that marked the fallen houses, her heart beat very fast. Here, not so long ago, other children had played. She recalled the story of Malinche. Here, like Malinche, her princess must have lived. She took Pancha's hand to make to-day seem more real. Together they looked in wonder at the huge stones, carved deep in fantastic designs, which formed the massive walls. Papa called to them to come with him to the platform above. At the corner, where the stairs used to be, he helped them over heaps of broken stone. Alejandro and his father followed with the picks, and began to turn up the loose earth. It was full of treasures, now a shining obsidian knife or arrowhead, keen as glass, now a face, roughly chiseled, no larger than one's finger. Other images in clay there were, and many little disks with holes in them which papa explained had been used in twisting thread.

"Did they use to spin here?" asked Pancha.

"Not right here, for this was a temple. See, this block of stone where we are putting our idols and things, was the altar. They used to worship the sun."

Just then Alejandro called. He had found a column so tipped as to be sheltered from the weather. On the under part of it, plain to be seen if one stooped, was the print of a small, red hand.

"What is that, señor?"

"That," cried papa, "is a treasure worth more than this whole mound put together! See, it is hardly larger than Lucita's hand, but that was the imprint of either the man who owned or the man who built this temple—of the king, or of his architect. Warm and alive, he put his hand there, dipped in the blood of his sacrifice. We, hundreds of years later, come upon his seal. All the old ruins have just such hands, placed beside the door. That, Alejandro, is the hand of one of our ancestors, yours and mine."

"Yes, señor," said the boy reverently; "only, señor, even then your fathers ruled over mine."

Don Hilario's hand rested for a moment on the boy's head. "It is true, and that is why my Alejandro makes such a faithful servant, and can be trusted with all I have."

"I wonder," said Lucita softly, "why they went away, the people of this wonderful city. Why did they not live in their old palaces?"

"No one will ever know. All over our country stand these ruins, with no history except tradition and what we can guess from their silent walls. Come, it is time to go down to lunch."

Soberly and yet happily the children clambered down. Under the trees, not far away, Aunt Stasia and Don Enrique had spread the luncheon, while mamma and Doña Felicia napped cozily in hammocks swung in the shade. They woke, however, to the clatter and the chatter of the children, and afterward they, too, went exploring up on the old, gray mound.

Then, in the cool of the evening, the horses were headed toward home. As Lucita looked back, the rising moon touched with magic the site of the ancient city, and seemed to wake it to life. In the shadows, were there not figures crouching? She could almost see them, winding upward to the temple where stood the priest, his arms raised in blessing to the sky.

XIII

AT THE FORGE

IT was at sunset on the following day that the children stopped to watch José working at the forge. He did not usually work so late, but this was a special order he was filling for Alejandro, he explained. At this, Alejandro showed all his white teeth in happy laughter, and Lucita, and Pancha, too, seemed to understand and approve. For Alejandro wanted some day to be an engineer; not an engineer like papa, but one who runs a locomotive. Every day when the up-train and the down-train from the city were due, Alejandro pattered over to the platform, and climbed aboard the engine for the few minutes of its stay. He watched, with curious, quick eyes, the wheels and the levers, and he listened when the American fireman good-naturedly explained their uses. Once, seeing the boy's interest, the fireman prevailed on the engineer to take him along to the next station. That was a great occasion. It was then that Alejandro knew in his heart what he was going to be.

Alejandro's father was no ordinary Indian. In the years of his master's prosperity he had been his *mozo* and traveled about with him. In this way he had seen much of machinery, and had come to realize how important it was to understand it. There was machinery everywhere, at the mines, in the cities, on the farms. Why, even here, in quiet San Angel, was not the master about to harness the water, and build a great mill, and lay miles and miles of railroad all his own? He was pleased indeed at the turn Alejandro's fancy had taken. With more boys like him in Mexico, the days of the foreign engineers and electricians and directors would soon be over. And so, when Alejandro began the making of a toy engine, as much like a real one as he could get it, he was not scolded. On the contrary, his father told him he would help him with it. That was what he was doing now.

The coals in the fire burned brightly, blown upon by the bellows, almost too large for Alejandro's arms to wield. The hammer fell swiftly on the red-hot iron that was being fashioned into tiny shafts and couplings by José's skillful strokes. The boiler, already completed, stood firmly on its wooden wheels; box cars and flat cars made quite a train behind it. Lucita and Pancha examined them in wonder and admiration.

"Why, Alejandro, when did you have time to do all this?" Lucita asked.

"In the mornings, mostly, before you were up, and at night, too, like this. I meant to surprise you with more, but the Señorita Pancha is going away so soon I could not wait."

"Yes, so soon," repeated Pancha sadly; "to-morrow, they say. So I'm glad you let us come to-night."

"To-morrow!" echoed Lucita in dismay. "Why, how can you go until your uncle comes back?"

"But he will be back; I overheard your papa tell Aunt Felicia. He is hurrying, and he will be here to-night. President Diaz is coming for a hunting trip and wants him to go along."

"President Diaz coming!" exclaimed José. "That is good news indeed!"

"But aren't you a little sorry he is coming so soon, because I have to go away?" Pancha looked at José in mock displeasure. "I haven't even heard the story you promised to tell me the very first night I came."

"He shall tell it now. Won't you, Uncle José?"

José paused in his turning and hammering. His brown eyes rested very kindly on the three children. "I did not think you would care so much for an old man's stories. What shall it be, *niña?* Shall I tell you of Brother Iguana and the Rabbit, or of Prince Eagle and the Flower of the Moon?"

Pancha considered. Alejandro whispered his vote for Brother Iguana, but Lucita waited for Pancha to speak. "I think," she said at last, "I think I'd like to hear about Prince Eagle."

"I think perhaps you all would, because it tells, too, of the times before the conquerors came, the times when people lived in cities like the one you visited yesterday. Only this happened not here, but in the City of Mexico, where President Diaz lives now."

The children seated themselves in a circle about the dying fire, which Alejandro forgot to blow. Only José, now and then, picked a red-hot bit of iron from the coals, and hammered very softly as he spoke.

"I am going to tell you, my dear little listeners," he began, "a story both tender and moving, in which are recited the adventures of an Aztec prince, called Sir Eagle. The tale is tender because this Sir Eagle saved from a death of terrible torture a young Aztec maiden, whose poetic name was 'Flor de Luna,' which means 'The Flower of the Moon.'

"A soldier in the armies of the King of Tenochtitlan (as the Valley of Mexico was then called) was the father of the lovely Flor de Luna. Her mother, when she was born, took in her hands a pomegranate and a tiny glass of copal, murmuring, 'Oh, Flor de Luna, child of my love and of my sufferings, I desire that the first years of thy life should be dedicated to the service of the temple, where are worshiped the gods who have the power to make happy and prosperous the people of Mexico.'

"The girl entered the temple as a priestess, attracting attention by her beauty. She passed her days spinning cotton, embroidering with finest feathers the robes of the king, cleaning the armor (made of the skins of tigers or serpents) which belonged to the youths of the College of War. There, while they were really only children, the lads learned the art of war. At night, all alone in a large and heavy canoe, the girl went to fish in the most lonely places on the lake, to bring to the priests their food for the following day.

"What unbounded admiration had the young warriors, who were being educated in the college, for Flor de Luna! Much they loved her already, and dreamed how one day they would marry her! But her older companions, who envied and did not like her, were always saying terrible things about her, telling the priests that she was an impostor who pretended humility and devotion when she went at night to fish or to bring wood and reeds from the shores of the lake. The child wept bitterly when she was reprimanded by the cruel priests. But one of them said to her:

" 'That you may show us that you do not go to plot treasons with the low people of the market place, or that you do not go to the Field of Flowers, where they give you in exchange for your perfidies the beautiful fish which you bring us a little before the great sun rises between the giants of rock that guard our city—Popocatepetl and Ixtaccihuatl—that you may prove to us, O bold Flor de Luna, that you are no traitor, bring to us this same night, instead of flowers, canes, and fish, three white herons, three black stags, and three wolves, half black, half white.'

" 'O my lord, great lord, great priest,' protested poor little Flor de Luna, crying bitterly, 'how am I alone, who have nothing but my canoe, my net, and my knife—how am I alone to get those creatures so wild, that fly so high, that run so fast, and that are so fierce? To get three white herons in a night, to catch three black stags, and to bring those three wolves—I, who have never seen one! How is it possible to do all that?'

" 'Only in this way can you save your life from the terrible torture that awaits the traitor,' answered the horrible old priest, furious in truth because a child so lovely as Flor de Luna should do such wonderful things as every one saw she did.

" 'I will go, my lord,' replied the unhappy maiden.

"They took, that night, a canoe very broad and long, to accommodate the three herons, the three stags, and the three

"They began to row over the black waters of the lake" Page 83

wolves that the poor girl had to bring—and she scarcely fifteen years old! There went in the canoe also two old and stout rowers, slaves, who were charged to do nothing but row wherever Flor de Luna required, without assisting her in the least in the terrible things she had to do. They began to row over the black waters of the lake, the girl standing in the middle of the boat, looking toward the black shadows of the mountains in the east. She was not crying now, but thinking of something very far away, and directing the rowers from time to time. What did the maiden at that instant hear?

"It was a song, rare and melodious, and thus it ran:

> " 'Fear not for thyself the fate
> A good genius shows thee;
> Spirit of the mountains yonder
> Who adores thee, Flor de Luna.
> Follow where the summits wait
> For thy coming. There shall be
> Thy Protector, who will give,—
> If thou look on him as purely
> As the Gods would wish,—ah, surely
> He will give thee with the herons
> All the life thou fain wouldst live.'

"What a cry of joy the poor child gave to hear this song! She was saved! She knew that a mighty genius of the enchanted islands, where dwelt the spirit of the Mother of the Gods, was protecting her. But who was the warrior of whom the mysterious song told her, who lived indeed on the peak to which she was going? Who was he? Who should he be? Trembling with doubts, she continued until the canoe was stopped by the tall reeds that grew at the mouth of the lake. There all was silence; not a bird, not a murmur of water, not a cry, not a human voice did she hear. Where was the warrior? In vain she waited long for some sound that might make her believe in the hero who was to aid her; nothing, not a murmur, not an echo. It seemed as if the world were dead.

"At last she despaired, lifting her arms to heaven and beating her breast and crying, 'O Mother, Mother Moon, save me! If thou dost not illumine the night, an innocent girl, who has adored the glory of thy light, will perish. Save me!'

"Scarcely had she spoken when suddenly, afar off, appeared a rosy radiance that presently turned to yellow; soon, round and enormous, rose the moon, and at the same moment a voice was heard which said:

" 'Glory to the Moon, and glory to thee, my love. I have come to thee, and I will save thee. I am Sir Eagle. I was trained in the College of War, and in the nights when we sallied forth to hunt men or beasts, in the marshes of the lake or in the mountains, I saw thee, lovely, fragile, and alone, fishing in these waters. I loved thee. I went with the veteran warriors to the campaigns, and I have taken so many captives that I am already Sir Eagle, as you see. To-day, wandering on the mountains, I wanted to sleep; in dreams a beautiful woman appeared to me who said: "If thou wishest to have Flor de Luna to wife, catch three herons, three stags, and three wolves, and take them to-night to the shores of the lake, and wait." '

"'Then thou art my savior!' exclaimed the joyful Flor de Luna.

"'Yes—take me—' replied the warrior, and with a leap he sprang toward the canoe, where the maiden awaited him with open arms.

"The moon darkened, the three white herons turned black, the stags became white, and the wolves changed the color of their skins to green and red, and the canoe stirred to a greater force than the old rowers possessed.

"'What is it?' asked the astonished youth.

"'Ah, now I understand,' replied Flor de Luna; 'it is because thou art forbidden to me. I belong to the temple. If thou followest me farther, thou art lost. Go, to fight for our nation. I will do my duty as a priestess of the temple, and soon our king, and my venerable parents, will reward thy labors and my sacrifices, by giving us to each other in marriage. Farewell!'

"But Sir Eagle replied not; he threw himself into the waters of the lake and, swimming, disappeared.

"Then the canoe followed its course to Tenochtitlan. The three herons, the three stags, and the three wolves changed to their original colors, the moon appeared, and so Flor de Luna came triumphant to the temple. There the priests, marveling, believed her to be the daughter of the gods themselves, and went and told the miracle to the king. He, with the consent of her parents, gave her as a wife to the brave warrior, Sir Eagle, when he returned victorious from his next campaign."

By the time the story ended the fire in the forge had burned to ashes, and swift shadows had fallen upon the valley. The children said good night; Lucita and Pancha to go to sleep in their little white beds, and Alejandro to curl up beside his father on the floor.

XIV

THE PRESIDENT'S HUNT

PANCHA was right. President Diaz was coming on a hunting trip. He was coming to the Hacienda of San Angel. Not that he would stay at the house, oh, no, he was too much of a sportsman for that. He and his party would stop only long enough to take horses, and then push on to a camp some twelve miles away. Great was the excitement at the Hacienda, however, and equally great the disappointment when the president's secretary wrote that his Excellency could not think of putting them to the trouble of preparing a dinner for so large a party as his. It seems he used to know Don Hilario in the old days in Mexico City, and had a very genuine regard for him.

But Don Hilario, on his part, could not let the president, whom every Mexican honored, pass through his small domain without some sign of welcome. Doña María and Aunt Anastasia and he consulted together.

"We will decorate the station," they said finally, "and serve a little luncheon there."

Fifty Indians were taken from the fields, and set to work under Don Enrique's direction to gather fruits and greens and flowers. They heaped ripe pumpkins and squashes and ears of red and yellow corn in a huge pile upon the platform. They made a great basket of green willow withes, and filled it with *chirimoyas*, and figs, and oranges, and pomegranates, and many strange tropic fruits. They cased the pillars in fanlike palmettos, and broad sheafs of banana leaves. They draped between them the national colors, green and white and red. At one end of the platform a bougainvillæa vine formed a bower. Beneath it a table was laid. Poinsettias, cosmos, heliotrope, roses, lilies, and a dozen bright-hued flowers were woven into screens or placed in vases. The gray station looked like a fairy's palace.

So Lucita thought when she came down, on the morning the president's train was expected, to help Aunt Anastasia carry the last load of dainty glassware from the house. Mamma was not coming until later, but Lucita was to have a very important part in the occasion, and had to know just what she was to do. If you had seen her I think you would have thought her a fairy worthy of her palace. All in white she was, of some filmy weave, except for a chain of gold and a pendant which hung about her neck. The pendant was a rose, cut in stone, a rose of light and fire, glowing like a live thing against her white dress. It was an opal, and had come from papa's mine.

Papa had come down early, too. He was at one end of the platform, giving the last orders to the Indian who had charge of the horses the president and his party were to ride. Each horse, sleek as satin and decked with rosettes of green and white and red, and saddle blankets of gay colors, was held by a white-clad boy. One pony—yes, it was Lucita's—was in Alejandro's care. Beyond the horses the

Indians—men, women, and children—were gathering to see their president.

In spite of the excitement Lucita's eyes almost filled as she saw Pajarito there. She left Aunt Anastasia and walked over to papa, and slipped her hand in his.

"He will be good to my pony, will he not, papa?" she asked anxiously.

Papa looked down at her quickly. "If you are going to worry, dearie, we will give the prince another mount," he said.

"No, no," protested Lucita. "I want him to have Pajarito—only I—I think I shall miss him. And of course he will be good to my horse," she continued, stroking the pony's soft white nose.

It was the prince, I am afraid, that Lucita was thinking of more than of the president, as she conned the little speech of welcome she was to make. Yes, the same prince who had once played with her in the garden in Rosario was coming with the president to-day. He had said he would not forget his princess. But would he recognize her here? Lucita looked almost regretfully at her lovely dress. If they had only let her wear her old gingham! And yet, she wanted to look lovely, too.

Mamma came at last, in Don Enrique's new carriage. Together the family stood in a group on the platform as the train drew in. Soldiers in the uniform of the *rurales* dismounted first. They formed a passageway from the steps to the waiting group. Other soldiers began to unload the dogs and the camping kits from the baggage car, and to hand the bundles for the pack horses to the waiting Indians. Those Indians who were not busy—and who on the Hacienda had not taken a holiday to-day?—pressed closer. From the platform stepped a white-haired, erect gentleman, whose keen eyes took in the scene at a glance. With bared heads, but with no other demonstration, the Indians greeted him. Don Hilario came forward, and the two men met, with a simple handclasp, as if the president were just an ordinary man after all.

That he was not, and that he had fought for and made this great republic in which she lived, Lucita knew. She felt a thrill of pride when he placed his hand on her head. But at the same time he looked at her so kindly that she quite forgot her little speech. With an impulse to give him the best she had, to render him the homage of her heart, she unclasped the chain from her neck, and laid it in his hands.

"Those Indians who were not busy . . . pressed closer"

For a moment, President Diaz looked bewildered.

Doña María came to the rescue. "It is for you, Excellency—a child's gift to her president."

When Lucita recovered from her confusion she found herself sitting at the table, at the president's right hand. Not only so, but opposite her sat the prince. And the president seemed to be making some very laughable remarks to papa, and to the rest of the company, about a certain occasion when the prince and Lucita had met before, and about a certain tree, called the "Tree of the Angels' Hair."

Lucita stole a look at the prince. He was laughing, too, right into her eyes. Evidently he enjoyed this second meeting as much as he had the first—and he hadn't forgotten at all.

As soon as he had a chance, while the horses were being looked over, he told her eagerly of the many places he had visited since that spring day in Rosario, and of the hunt which was to end his trip. By the next steamer he was going home.

"And you," he ended, "will you not be coming to Austria some day? I shall want to see you there."

"Thank you," said Lucita soberly. "Some day, when I am grown up, perhaps I will come to play with you there."

As Lucita lay awake that night, picture after picture of the day's adventures was thrown on the darkness of her quiet room. Once again she saw the *jefe* and his soldiers escorting the president from the train. She saw the laughing eyes of the prince, his pleasure at the sight of Pajarito, and the gallant way in which he mounted and swung off his hat in farewell. She recalled every look of President Diaz, who had lingered to say a real good-by to her. What was it he said? That he was taking her opal for his wife to wear? Yes, and that some day she must come to visit her.

At last the pictures blurred and faded, and Lucita fell asleep. But in her dreams she could not forget. Once more she played with the prince in the garden. Only, the garden belonged to President Diaz, and the prince turned out to be, in very truth, the little brother she had wanted all her life.

XV

LITTLE BROTHER

IN the weeks that followed the president's return Lucita was very much occupied. There were lessons now, every day, for the household work was running more smoothly for Aunt Anastasia, and the novelty of living in the country was wearing off. Lucita was not any less happy; she enjoyed her books, and she enjoyed, too, the little sewing tasks that she had to do. Perhaps if the tasks had been darning stockings, or piecing squares into quilts, she might not have enjoyed them. But they were not; not at all.

You see, Christmas was coming, and this year not even papa was going up to the city for presents. So, of course, presents had to be made; presents for papa, and mamma, and Aunty Stasia, and Petra, and Alejandro, and for some one else as well. They were all done except the last, and that was—what do you think? A tiny white petticoat, no bigger than a doll's! Its bottom was turned up in a hem, and at the top of this hem was a narrow, lacy band. The band was what Lucita was making, very slowly, very carefully, under Aunt Stasia's eye. First, she had pulled the threads that ran across the cloth. Then, over a little frame, she fastened in clusters those that were left and bound them together to make a pattern like lace. If she hadn't studied her arithmetic she could not have done it, because she had to count the threads. And she

There on Petra's knee lay Little Brother, fast asleep   Page 99

had to be very patient, for such an impatient little girl. In and out, in and out, wove her needle, making for "Little Brother" something she hoped he would like.

This was to be a very quiet Christmas at the Hacienda. The only guest who was expected, besides Little Brother, was Don Enrique. In the Indian village on the hill, to be sure, there would be a whole week of celebrating, with bull fights, and fireworks, and a procession to the ruined church, where the priest would say mass. On Christmas night the church would be illuminated by pitch-pine torches, and at dawn on Christmas morning the Indian women would go, singing, to hail the new-born Christ. But the Christmas at the master's house this year was to be an Americanized Christmas, with a turkey and a plum pudding and a genuine Christmas tree! Usually, instead of a tree, a large jar like a sugar mold was hung to hold the presents. Then every night, for nine nights, there were dances, and on Christmas Eve a kind of blind man's buff, in which the jar was broken and the presents showered down. Lucita could remember such Christmases in the city, when the house was full of guests. She was thinking of them as she worked out on the gallery this quiet afternoon. Except for the drowsy hum of bees among the flowers, and Chiquito's occasional song, there was not a sound to be heard. Every one else was asleep. But Christmas was only a week off, and the petticoat must be done.

By and by Aunt Stasia came out of her room, and sat down beside her. "How would you like to go up to Rosario with me to-morrow, Little Light?" she asked.

"To Rosario!" echoed Lucita in amazement.

"Yes," said she. "I find I have some shopping to do after all; something for that wonderful tree, and something for me, and, maybe, something for you. Would you like to go with aunty and stop at a real hotel, and surprise Carmen and Pancha and every one?"

"Could we come back in time?"

"In time for Christmas? Why, of course. Will you go with me?" And she swung Lucita into a happy little dance that ended in Lucita's bedroom, where they looked over her clothes together.

A linen dress, a pongee coat, and a Panama hat were laid out to wear on the train. Mamma came in for a minute, and smiled at Lucita's happy face. Aunt Stasia looked happy, too. Lucita thought she never had seen her so happy. And as for mamma, of course she was happy. Who would not be with such a Christmas present as she was going to have?

It was only papa who seemed a little worried and a little lonely as he took Lucita on his knee that night. "So," he said, "my little girl is going away from me to-morrow."

"But I'm coming back again soon, papa; and aunty is going with me," answered Lucita, who began to feel a little lonely herself. She had never been away from home before.

Papa saw the tears beginning to gather. "Why, of course, dear," he smiled; "and you will see so many pretty things and so many happy people that you'll be as happy as a thrush yourself. Besides, there will be lots of children you know, and some one else from home too."

"Who?"

"Don Enrique is going on the same train," said papa. Lucita thought he looked at Aunt Anastasia as he spoke. Certainly Aunt Stasia's cheeks grew quite pink. Lucita wondered why.

The next day they went away. Papa waved from the platform, and Lucita waved back as long as she could see him. The car was crowded. From the racks swayed baskets of oranges and bananas and garlands of bright flowers. Orange blossoms and cape jasmine made the air heavy with fragrance. Everybody was talking and laughing, for everybody was going somewhere to enjoy the Christmas holidays. Aunt Stasia and Don Enrique talked and laughed with the rest. They talked to Lucita, too, and bought her flowers and fruit from the Indian women at the stations, and tried to make her forget that she was going away from home. As the train neared Rosario they could see the familiar plantations, the palace, and the domes and towers of the cathedral crowning the hill above. No, Lucita could not feel homesick any longer, for here, too, she was at home.

The hotel, kept by an old school friend of Aunt Stasia's, Lucita had seen before only from the outside. As the carriage stopped at the entrance it looked very large and imposing to her. Up the broad stairs and along a wide arcade they went, until they came to a room at the very end. The maid threw open the door. Opposite, through a vine-fringed window, they looked straight out over the plain to the white cone of Popocatepetl. From another window they saw the court below, where the orange trees were in full flower. The pink walls, the brass beds, the white, clean covers, made a pretty, homelike picture. Lucita's last trace of homesickness vanished.

"Oh, aunty, weren't you good to bring me?" she said.

Aunt Stasia smiled. "We shall have a good time together, and have many things to tell when we get home."

Before dinner, that very night, Lucita saw all her old playmates, Pancha and Carmen and Pablo and Dick. They came to a tea Aunt Stasia gave for them in the *patio*. Pancha had told them a good deal about the Hacienda, but there were many more things they wanted to know.

"My," said Dick, when he heard of the Indian raid, "I'd like to live down there!"

"And did you say," asked Pablo, "that you were going to have a railroad all your own?"

"Yes, it is being built now, a tiny railroad, but big enough to carry cane to the mill. The mill is begun already. It stands away from the house, down by the stream."

"I'd like to see your chickens," said Carmen. "I think they're more fun than mills."

"But they aren't more fun than the stream," interrupted Dick. "Lucita was telling before you came how they go in swimming there."

Lucita laughed. "Yes; and of how Alejandro had to rescue me. Next year you must all come down, and I'll show you everything."

The days in the city flew by. Every morning, at the market or in the shops, Aunt Stasia bought trinkets for the tree, or pretty trifles for presents, or, most absorbing of all, yards and yards of dainty lawns and linens and laces. Why she should want so many, Lucita could not understand. Every afternoon, when the band played, she and Aunt Stasia and Don Enrique walked or sat in the Plaza. And every evening, dressed in her prettiest gowns, Aunt Stasia tripped away to some party on Don Enrique's arm. It was all very gay after the quiet life of the Hacienda; even at night you went to sleep to music, and wakened long afterward to hear it playing still.

But the day before Christmas found Lucita and Aunt Stasia once more at home. The house seemed far more quiet than before. Mamma had been sick, papa said, but she was better now, and would like to see her

In the market

little girl. So Lucita tiptoed softly into mamma's room. Aunt Stasia was there before her, and evidently had been telling mamma something important, for mamma was saying, "Oh, Stasia, I am so glad, and I hope you will be as happy, as happy can be."

Lucita ran to her mother's side. "Please kiss me, mamma, because I've missed you. And why are you so happy?"

"Partly, dear, because your Aunt Stasia is going to marry Don Enrique, and partly— Come here, and I'll whisper it so even Aunt Stasia won't hear."

As she whispered, the perplexed look on Lucita's face changed to rapture. She didn't understand why one should be glad to marry Don Enrique, but she did understand this. More softly than she had come in, she tiptoed across the room. At the inner door she paused. A voice she knew, Petra's voice, was singing very low. And this is what she sang:

"Lullaby, my baby,
Lulla, lullaby.
Go to sleep, my baby,
Baby of my heart.

"Those two little brown eyes,
Thou hast shut them tight;
Eyes that when they're open
Are all my heart's delight.

"The glory they are singing,
Holy voices, to thee;
That thou mayst sleep sweetly,
Sweet dreams they are bringing.

"Sleep, sleep well, my baby,
Sleep, my baby boy,
Sleep within the shelter
Of my inmost heart.

"In the sky above,
There's a window high.
Leaneth down in love,
Blest Saint Anthony.

"In my sky below,
There are windows, too,
Eyelids opening slow
Let the lovelight through.

"Lullaby, my baby,
Lulla, lullaby.
Sent because I love thee,
Baby of my heart."

Little Light opened the door noiselessly and stole in. There on Petra's knee lay Little Brother—oh, such a *little* brother—fast asleep.

PETRA'S LULLABY

Arranged by R. P. Conkling

Lul - la - by, . . my ba - by, Lul - la, lul - la - by; . .

Go to sleep, . . my ba - by, Ba - by of my heart;

Ba - by, ba - by, Ba - by of my heart.

Those two lit - tle brown eyes Thou hast shut them tight;

Rit.

Eyes that when they're o - pen Are all my heart's de - light.

a tempo.

Lul - la - by, . . my ba - by, Lul - la, lul - la - by; . .

Go to sleep, . . my ba - by, Ba - by of my heart,

Rall. e dim.   *pp*

Ba - by, ba - by, Ba - by of my heart.

NOTES

PAGE LINE
1   5. *Tiles.* Thin pieces of baked clay used for roof, floors, or walls, especially in countries like Mexico, where wood is scarce.

1   5. *Lucita.* If you look in the Foreword you will see that Lucita is the diminutive, or pet name, for Luz, which means *light*. Mexico is a Roman Catholic country, and Our Lady of Light is one of the titles by which Mary, mother of Jesus, is best known, because she is wise and gives light for guidance in time of trouble. Each year a special day is set aside in the churches to tell the people about this. On one of these days Lucita was born; so her father and mother, instead of calling her Mary, called her Little Light.

1   8. *Patio.* A court, usually a pretty garden around which the Mexican house is built.

1   11. *Doña Marina.* Lady Marina; *doña* is the Spanish word for Lady.

2   10. *Anastasia.* Means "from the sea." The name is often shortened to Stasia. See p. 3.

2   14. *Rosario.* A city in the state of Morelos.

2   16. *Drawn work of linen.* Linen in which the crosswise threads are drawn to form a pattern. The lengthwise threads are then fastened into clusters with a needle, until the piece of drawn work looks like lace.

2   20. *Brocades from Japan.* You will like to read in this connection *The Lost Galleon*, by Bret Harte.

2   25. *Potteries.* Dishes made of coarse baked clay, usually coarser than china.

2   25. *Ware of Talavera and of Puebla.* Talavera was a city in Spain famous for its potteries. From Talavera potters came to teach the native potters of Puebla in Mexico how to make their ware. Some say that Chinese potters also came from China to help them, because the patterns they used are Chinese and because Mexico in those days traded with all those countries we know as the Far East.

NOTES

PAGE LINE

2 27. *Indian blankets.* The Indians, divided into many tribes like our Indians, now form the common people of Mexico. They are farmers, shop keepers, servants, and laborers. Most of them are part Spanish, but many of them are of pure Indian blood. They wear blankets, often beautifully colored and woven, in place of overcoats.

2 28. *Joseph's coat.* Do you know who Joseph was, and why his coat was so gay? You will find this story in the Old Testament, Genesis, xxxvii, 3.

3 9 *Doña María.* Spanish for Lady Mary.

3 12. *Austrian Minister.* Every nation has at the capital of every other nation a man who represents the government of his country. He is called a minister or an ambassador. The Austrian minister represented the government of Austria.

3 14. *Gallery.* A word used in the south in the sense of veranda. Here, the porch at the back of the *patio*.

3 18. *Tortillas.* A *tortilla* is a pancake, or an omelet.

3 25. *Tia.* The Spanish word for aunt.

4 4. *Chiquito.* Another diminutive, or pet name, meaning "very little."

4 9. *Balustrade.* A low railing. In Lucita's house it was made of concrete, and ran around the *patio*.

5 8. *Mango trees.* These trees grow to be very large, and have thick, glossy leaves. The fruit is yellow, sometimes with red cheeks like apples, and shaped like a long, flattened kind of peach.

5 11. *Coffee bushes.* Coffee is the seed of a red berry growing on bushes. Mexican coffee is very choice.

5 15. *Wicket.* A small gate.

6 3. *Mirador.* A pavilion or summerhouse.

6 10. *Bastions.* A bastion is a platform projecting beyond a castle wall.

6 14. *Empress Carlota.* Carlota was the wife of the Archduke Maximilian of Austria. At the time of our Civil War Maximilian was made Emperor of Mexico by Napoleon III of France. When the Civil War was over, our country demanded that the French withdraw from Mexico. They did so in 1866, and abandoned

NOTES

PAGE LINE

        Maximilian, who was shot by a Mexican army. His wife, the beautiful Carlota, was crazed with grief.

7   3. *De Alarcón.* The name of a noble and famous Spanish family.

7 11. *Caballero.* A gentleman. In Mexico the owners of land are looked on much as nobles are in Europe. Lucita's father was a landowner.

7 12. *Americana.* An American lady.

7 28. *President Diaz.* The President of Mexico from 1877 to 1880, and from 1884 to 1910.

8 10. *Chapultepec.* The summer home of the Mexican presidents. Before the Spaniards conquered Mexico the palace of the Aztec, or Indian, emperors stood in the same beautiful spot.

10 3. *Pancha de Herrera.* Pancha is the diminutive of Francisca, as Lucita is of Luz.

10 5. *Pablo.* Spanish for Paul.

10 9. *Turistas.* The meaning of tourist I think you know. A *turista* is a lady tourist; the men do not usually care to ride donkeys. The use of this word is confined to Mexico.

11 1. *Niñita.* Little girl.

11 8. *Catalina.* Spanish for Catherine.

12 3. *Convent.* The home of nuns. In this convent the nuns taught school.

12 5. *Vender.* A man who peddles. The Mexican vender of candies spreads the candies on a tray which has supports like a camp stool so that it can be set up anywhere he chooses.

12 7. *Buenos dias.* Spanish for "Good day."

12 8. *Panadería el Vapor.* In English, the steam bakery! Every shop in Mexico has a name.

12 23. *Adiós.* Spanish for "Good-by."

12 26. *Plaza.* Every Mexican city and village has its central square or park, called the plaza.

12 27. *Plane trees.* The plane tree is much prized in hot countries because of its wide-spreading branches and deep shade.

13 1. *Juan.* Spanish for John.

13 11. *Cobbled street.* A street paved with small, round stones. It makes a good street for a country where the people ride horseback as much as they do in Mexico; but it is very rough for a carriage.

NOTES

PAGE LINE
- **14 7.** *Thursday.* Thursday and Sunday are usually the busiest market days of the week.
- **14 12.** *Tamales.* A hash made of meat, corn meal, and peppers, wrapped in a corn husk.
- **14 17.** *Fluted glass.* Glass molded in parallel grooves.
- **14 18.** *Red-lacquered gourds.* Gourds grow on vines and look something like squashes, but the rind is hard. From them dishes are made and covered with lacquer or varnish.
- **14 24.** *Stenciled.* A stencil is a decoration printed in dots and lines.
- **14 25.** *Ollas.* Earthen pots or jugs.
- **14 27.** *Brasero.* A brazier or pan for holding hot coals.
- **15 16.** *Hempen bags.* Hemp is made from the fibers of a plant. One of the best hemps, known as sisal hemp, is grown in the state of Yucatan, Mexico.
- **15 26.** *Presto.* A word that jugglers used long ago to call attention to their tricks, which people then thought were magical. So we use it for something that startles us because it seems impossible or very wonderful.
- **17 1.** *Lucita mia.* My Little Light.
- **17 9.** *Bougainvillæa.* A vine with purple, pink, red, or yellow foliage, according to its varieties. It is said the Empress Carlota brought it with her from her home in Italy. It has become very common in Mexico.
- **17 22.** *Carita.* Little dear, or darling.
- **19 5.** *Conquistador.* The title, meaning conqueror, by which Cortés is best known.
- **19 6.** *Cortés.* Hernando Cortés was born in the fifteenth century in Spain. With an army of about six thousand five hundred men he conquered Mexico, as the story tells you.
- **19 19.** *Pretty feathers.* The Indians of Mexico, or Aztecs as they were called, made the feathers of humming birds and parrots into material for dresses and hangings. They raised the birds in large numbers for this purpose.
- **20 24.** *Jungle.* A forest choked with undergrowth.
- **21 5.** *Chaplet.* A wreath.

NOTES

PAGE LINE
21 23. *Headdress.* See *Chaplet.*
22 2. *Yucatan.* The southeasternmost state of Mexico.
22 3. *Cuba.* Columbus discovered this island, and it belonged to Spain from 1492 until 1896.
22 11. *Montezuma.* He was the last Indian, or Aztec, emperor.
22 14. *Dally.* Play, in the sense of fool with.
24 13. *Popocatepetl.* An Indian name meaning "Smoking Mountain." It does not smoke now.
24 13. *Ixtaccihuatl.* An Indian name meaning "The White Woman." The Indians thought the outline of the mountain looked like a sleeping woman. They said she was the wife of Popocatepetl.
24 16. *Maguey.* What we call the "century plant." In Mexico it is cultivated, and its juice made into a drink something like beer.
25 14. *Dais.* A platform.
26 1. *Granary.* A storehouse for grain.
26 2. *Ingots.* Bars of gold.
27 5. *Fiesta.* A festival, or holiday.
27 7. *Saint Francis.* St. Francis de Sales, or San Francisco as he is called in Spanish, is the saint on whose day Francisca was born. He lived about three hundred years ago. Every child who is named after him tries to imitate him in keeping his temper under control.
27 22. *Mantilla.* A lace scarf or shawl thrown over the head in place of a hat.
28 24. *Oleanders.* Shrubs which have glossy leaves and fragrant, rose-colored flowers.
28 24. *Crêpe myrtles.* Evergreen shrubs, something like oleanders. The blossoms are pinker, and crinkled like crêpe.
29 3. *Portulacas.* These flowers look something like primroses but are of all shades of yellow, pink, and red. They grow close to the ground.
30 22. *Landaus.* Open carriages with very low bodies, so that they are easy to step into.
31 3. *Cavalcade.* A company of riders.
31 21. *Sluiceways.* Channels or ditches for running water. As the part of Mexico where Lucita lives has little rain, water from springs or rivers is carried for miles in sluiceways to water the crops.

NOTES

PAGE LINE
32 20. *Nieve.* This means snow, and is the Mexican word for ice cream.
33 3. *Gracias.* Thanks.
33 3. *Niña.* This means girl, but it is used to older women very respectfully, like a title.
33 24. *Mama mia.* Can you not guess what these words mean?
34 8. *Haciendas.* An *hacienda* is a very large plantation, sometimes many miles in extent.
34 14. *Knickknacks.* Trinkets and inexpensive trifles.
34 17. *Images of Judas.* These are hanged to show contempt for Judas, who sold Jesus for money. They are fired off when the bells ring for the Resurrection because then Jesus triumphed over all his enemies.
35 6. *Canary Islands.* Islands off the coast of Africa belonging to Spain. The women of the islands are very skillful makers of lace and drawn work.
35 9. *Muleteer.* A man who drives a mule or donkey.
35 17. *Panniers.* Baskets fastened on both sides of a saddle, for carrying loads.
35 18. *San Cristóbal.* Spanish for St. Christopher.
35 21. *Don Enrique.* Don is the usual title of the landowner as *doña* is of his wife. Enrique is the Spanish word for Henry.
35 27. *Arcade.* An arched open passage or veranda.
36 2. *Opals.* These are precious stones, used for jewelry.
36 4. *Hilario.* Spanish for Hilary.
37 7. *Pobrecita.* A diminutive meaning "poor little thing."
38 11. *Holy Week.* The week beginning with Palm Sunday and ending with Easter.
38 25. *Te Deum laudamus.* These Latin words, meaning "Thee, Lord, we praise," begin the musical service of the Catholic church called the mass.
38 27. *The glory.* From the figures above the altar spreads a gilded aureole, as if the glory of God shone out in that way. This aureole is called the glory.
42 14. *Jasmine.* A small, white, wax-like flower, very fragrant.
46 1. *Hot country.* Mexico, owing to differences in elevation above sea

NOTES

PAGE LINE

level, has many differences in climate. Up on the table-lands it is cool or cold, but down on the lower lands, or on the coast, the weather is always warm. This latter region is called the hot country.

46 2. *Battlemented.* In old times a castle usually had a wall about its roof or towers, with loopholes through which the soldiers could shoot their arrows. These walls were called battlements.

46 3. *San Angel.* This really means St. Angel, or Holy Angel.

47 9. *Major-domo.* The overseer of a house or an estate.

47 15. *Buzzards.* These birds are a kind of large hawk.

48 21. *Ricebirds.* These are small black birds which get their name because they feed on the rice harvests.

49 12. *Alligator pear.* A fruit shaped like a huge green pear, but eaten as a vegetable.

51 8. *José.* Spanish for Joseph.

51 8. *Tomas.* Spanish for Thomas.

53 14. *Señorita.* This pretty word means "Miss"; but Doña María's servants call her so in compliment, as if they should say, "You are not really old enough to be married."

56 7. *Oasis.* A green spot in a desert fed by springs.

56 7. *Royal palms.* A very tall and beautiful kind of palm tree.

57 19. *Pajarito.* A diminutive, meaning "Little Bird."

58 2. *Cactus hedges.* Mexico has many different varieties of cactus. Some are trained into hedges for protection, and on account of their sharp thorns make very good fences.

58 16. *Irrigating ditch.* See *Sluiceway*, p. 106.

59 27. *Cañon.* A ravine, the walls of which are very steep.

59 28. *Covey.* A flock.

60 5. *Iguana.* A kind of lizard.

60 23. *Pedro.* Spanish for Peter.

62 4. *Well his ancestors used.* Mexico is a volcanic country. In such a country there are likely to be underground caves containing pools of water and rivers. The Indians went to these springs or rivers for water because they often had no other water supply.

64 19. *Las Palmillas.* Diminutive of *palmas*, meaning palms; here the name of a village.

NOTES

PAGE LINE
65 2. *Earthquake.* In Mexico earthquakes are common. Sometimes they do a great deal of damage.
65 12. *Vicente.* Spanish for Vincent.
65 15. *Dolores.* She was born on Good Friday, which is known in Mexico as the day of Our Lady of Sorrows. Is not Sorrows a strange name for a little girl?
67 9. *Panchita.* Little Pancha or Frances.
67 10. *Amiga.* Friend.
68 7. *Jefe político.* Head official of a district.
68 15. *Aqueducts.* In bringing water for irrigating puposes it sometimes had to be carried over a valley. A bridge for it was then built called an aqueduct.
69 27. *Doña Felicia.* This name means happiness.
70 3. *Aguardiente.* "Fire water," alcohol.
71 6. *Bandits.* Armed robbers or highwaymen.
74 2. *Atlan.* The name of an ancient ruined town.
75 2. *Ruiz de Alarcón.* One of Cortés's soldiers.
75 21. *Cosmos.* A star-like flower, white or pink. It blossoms in the fall.
75 21. *Coreopsis.* A flower with yellow ruffled petals and a brown velvety center.
76 11. *Obsidian.* A black glass formed in the hot craters of volcanoes.
76 13. *Disk.* A round, flat plate. These disks were about an inch across. They were fastened to one end of the flax fiber, which was twisted into a thread by the spinning weight.
78 19. *Mozo.* A man servant.
80 28. *Aztec.* The native Indians of Mexico, before the Spanish conquest, are called Aztecs.
81 4. *Tenochtitlan.* The Indian or Aztec name for the City of Mexico.
81 7. *Pomegranate.* A fruit shaped like a rose hip, only much larger. When it is ripe it bursts open, showing its pink flesh and white seeds.
81 7. *Copal.* This is a valuable gum which was used by the Aztecs as money, or tribute. Flor de Luna's mother offered it to the gods.
82 6. *Field of Flowers.* An Aztec city across the lake from Tenochtitlan. In the lake before the city were many "floating gardens," or huge

NOTES

PAGE LINE

rafts, bright with growing flowers. So the lake, too, was called the Field of Flowers.

88 1. *Chirimoyas.* Custard apples. They look something like greenings, but are filled with a soft pulp that tastes like a pineapple custard.

88 3. *Palmettos.* These trees are not so tall as palms and have fan-shaped leaves from which fans are made.

88 6. *Poinsettias.* Brilliant scarlet flowers with long pointed petals and yellow centers.

93 7. *Bullfights.* These are games between men and bulls which are usually very wild and fierce. Crowds go to see the game, much as we go to see a game of baseball.

93 17. *Christmas Eve.* In Mexico Christmas Eve is called "The Good Night" (*La Noche Buena*).

94 12. *Panama hat.* A hat of fine straw woven by hand in South America.

98 15. *The Glory.* This is a Latin hymn, but you can find the English words in St. Luke. It is the song the angels sang to the shepherds on the first Christmas Eve.

98 26. *Saint Anthony.* St. Anthony of Padua, in Italy, was known everywhere for his love of children.

A READING LIST

ARNOLD, CHANNING, and FROST, FREDERICK J. TABOR. *The American Egypt; A Record of Travel in Yucatan.* New York: Doubleday, Page & Co. 1909.

AUDUBON, JOHN W. *Western Journal.* Cleveland: The Arthur H. Clark Company. 1906.

BANDELIER, A. F. *The Gilded Man (El Dorado), and Other Pictures of the Spanish Occupancy of America.* New York: D. Appleton and Company. 1893.

BARBER, EDWIN ATLEE. *Tin-enameled Pottery, Majolica, Delft, and Other Stainferous Faïence.* The Museum, Phila. Art Primer, Ceramic Series No. 5.

BARTON, MARY. *Impressions of Mexico with Brush and Pen.* New York: Macmillan & Company. 1911.

BIART, LUCIEN. *The Aztecs: Their History, Manners and Customs.* Translated from the French by J. L. Garner. Chicago: A. C. McClurg & Co. 1900.

CREELMAN, JAMES. *Diaz, Master of Mexico.* New York and London: D. Appleton and Company. 1911.

FLANDRAU, CHARLES MACOMB. *Viva Mexico!* New York: D. Appleton and Company, 1908.

HALE, SUSAN. *The Story of Mexico.* New York: G. P. Putnam's Sons. 1898.

HENTY, G. A. *By Right of Conquest; or, with Cortez in Mexico.* New York: Charles Scribner's Sons. 1900.

JANVIER, THOMAS A. *Legends of the City of Mexico.* New York and London: Harper & Brothers. 1910.

The Aztec Treasure-House; A Romance of Contemporaneous Antiquity. New York and London: Harper & Brothers. 1890.

KIRKHAM, STANTON DAVIS. *Mexican Trails.* New York and London: G. P. Putnam's Sons. 1909.

A READING LIST

LUMMIS, CHARLES F. *The Land of Poco Tiempo.* New York: Charles Scribner's Sons. 1893.
The Spanish Pioneers. Chicago: A. C. McClurg & Co. 1893.
MCDONALD, ETTA BLAISDELL, and DALRYMPLE, JULIA. *Manuel in Mexico.* Boston: Little Brown & Company. 1910.
MUNROE, KIRK. *The White Conquerors: a tale of Toltec and Aztec.* New York: Charles Scribner's Sons. 1893.
PRESCOTT, W. H. *History of the Conquest of Mexico.* Philadelphia: J. B. Lippincott Co. 1896.
SMITH, F. HOPKINSON. *A White Umbrella in Mexico.* Boston and New York: Houghton Mifflin & Co. 1899.
SMITH, NORA ARCHIBALD. *Under the Cactus Flag; A Story of life in Mexico.* Boston and New York: Houghton Mifflin & Co. 1899.
STEPHENS, JOHN L. *Incidents of Travel in Yucatan (rare).* New York: Harper & Brothers. 1868.
STODDARD, W. O. *The Lost Gold of the Montezumas; A Story of the Alamo.* Philadelphia: J. B. Lippincott Co. 1909.
TERRY, T. PHILIP. *Terry's Mexico. Handbook for Travellers.* Boston and New York: Houghton Mifflin & Co. 1911.
WALLACE, DILLON. *Beyond the Mexican Sierras.* Chicago: A. C. McClurg & Co. 1910.
WALLACE, LEW. *The Fair God; or, the Last of the 'Tzins: A Tale of the Conquest of Mexico.* Boston and New York: Houghton Mifflin & Co. 1905.

A GUIDE TO PRONUNCIATION

In indicating pronunciation, the usage of Mexico and South America, and not the Castillian usage, has been followed.

It should be borne in mind that the vowel sounds are prolonged and the consonants more softly pronounced than in English.

adiós (ah dē ōs')
aguardiente (ah gwar dē en'teh)
Alejandro (ah lĕ hahn'drō)
Americana (ah may rē kah'nah)
amiga (ah mē'gah)
Anastasia (ah nah stah'sē ah)
Antonia (ahn tō'nē ah)
Atlan (aht lahn')
bougainvillæa (boo gan vēl'yah)
brasero (brah say'ro)
buenos dias (bway'nōs dē'ahs)
caballero (kah bāl yay'ro)
cañon (kan yon')
carita (kah rē'tah)
Carlota (kar lŏ'tah)
Carmen Carrillo (car'men car rēl'yo)
Catalina (kah tah lē'nah)
Chapultepec (chah pool'tey pek)
Chiquito (chē kē'to)
chirimoyas (chē rē moi'yahs)
conquistador (kōn kēs'tah dor)
coreopsis (kō rē ŏp'sĭs)
Cortés, Hernando (ayr nahn'do kortes')
De Alarcón (day ah lar kon')
Diaz (dē'as)
Dolores (dō lōr'ays)
Don Enrique (dōn ĕn rē'keh)
Don Hilario (dōn ē lah'rē o)
Doña Felicia (dōn'yah fay lē'sē ah)
Doña María (dōn'yah mah rē'ah)
Doña Marina (dōn'yah mah rē'nah)
fiesta (fē es'tah)
Flor de Luna (flōr day loo'nah)
Francisca (fran sēs'kah)
gracias (grah'sē ahs)
hacienda (ah sē en'dah)
Iguana (ē gwah'nah)
Ixtaccihuatl (iss tas sē'watl)
jefe político (hay'fay pō lē'tē co)
José (hō say')
Juan (whahn)
la noche buena (lah nō'cheh bway'-nah)
Las Palmillas (lahs pahl mēl'yas)
Lucita (loo sē'tah)
Luz (loos)
maguey (mah gay')
Malinche (mah lĭn'cheh)
mama mia (mah'mah mē'ah)
mantilla (mahn tēl'yah)
mia (mē'ah)
mirador (mē rah dor')
Montezuma (mŏn teh zoo'mah)
morelos (mō ray'lōs)
mozo (mō'so)
nieve (nē ay'veh)
niña (neen'yah)
niñita (neen yē'tah)
olla (ōl'yah)
Pablo (pahb'lo)
Pajarito (pah hah rē'to)
Panadería el Vapor (pah nah dehrē'ah el vah por')
Pancha de Herrera (pahn'chah day ayr ray'rah)

A GUIDE TO PRONUNCIATION

Panchita (pahn chē'tah)
patio (pah'tē o)
Pedro (pay'dro)
plaza (plah'zah)
pobrecita (pō bray sē'tah)
Popocatepetl (pō pō cah'tē petl)
Puebla (pway'blah)
Quetzalcoatl (ket sahl'ko watl)
Rosario (rō sah'rē o)
Ruiz de Alarcón (roo ēs' day ah-lar kon')
rurale (roo rah'leh)

San Angel (sahn ahn'hayl)
San Cristóbal (sahn krēs tō'bahl)
señorita (sayn yo rē'tah)
Talavera (tah lah vay'rah)
tamale (tah mah'leh)
Tenochtitlan (teh nōk'tit lahn)
tia (tē'ah)
Tomas (tō mas')
tortilla (tor tēl'yah)
turista (too-rēs'tah)
Vicente (vē sĕn'teh)
Yucatan (yoo cah tahn')

SUGGESTIONS TO TEACHERS

THE aim of this story has been to make the little reader one of the happy home circle of a Mexican family of the better class. This class consists of the great landowners, descendants of the Spanish colonist nobles, who are virtually nobles still. Their sons and daughters are educated in Europe or America and in feelings live far removed from the Indians and more or less mixed races who perform the drudgery of the nation. Yet they understand these lower classes by long overlordship, as the Southern landowners did their slaves. And they entertain for them—with, of course, deplorable exceptions—the same patriarchal sentiments.

The Indians themselves, whose ancestors ruled the land before the Spaniards came, form an interesting study, and one that can be made to appeal especially to children. They are of many tribes and many customs. They are skillful in all painstaking handicrafts, lovers of music, of color, and of romance. They have an animal folklore very similar to that of the negroes. They cherish also the traditions of the Aztecs, though few of them have kept the freeborn spirit which is equally their right.

A conflict of races has been inevitable. But neither ancient wrongs nor the tyranny of the Diaz administration, shown to landowners and Indians alike, have dimmed the joyousness of the nation's normal life. The Mexican is accustomed to a land of political as well as of physical earthquakes. Sufficient unto each day is the pleasure thereof. The dark background, however, traced in the story in the confiscation of Don Hilario's mines and in "The Raid," the teacher will now have means to emphasize. Tranquility has not followed the overthrow of Diaz. President Madero is still grappling with the same problems his predecessor faced.

My feeling and the feeling of many well-informed students of Mexican history as to the former administration is this, that in the face of difficulties, internal and external, President Diaz raised Mexico with a strong

SUGGESTIONS TO TEACHERS

hand to a place among the nations of the world. His methods were autocratic, but necessarily so. At least, he made his Indian subjects happier than we have made ours. To him was due the excellent school system, the commercial development, the orderliness, and the good credit of Mexico. Whatever the future brings of advancement will be built on the foundations President Diaz laid. He has become a great historic figure, about whom American children ought to know.

But the different racial elements in Mexico point to another subject more pleasing and very dear to my heart. That is, the historical material of the story. Such legends as those of Malinche and Flor de Luna, and ruins like those of Atlan, are everyday facts to the average Mexican child. No one is a better authority on the Conquest than Prescott. Stephens—now unfortunately out of print—and Biart are equally authoritative in regard to the prehistoric civilizations. In this connection I want to suggest to teachers in the country that they can perhaps get the children interested in our own Indians as well as in the Indians of Mexico. In New England, in the South, and in the West arrowheads and Indian implements can be found right on their own farms. Spinning disks, I have been informed, are peculiar to Mexico and to Egypt—a little link in the chain of evidence archæologists are trying to forge between the builders of the Aztec and of the Egyptian pyramids.

If it seems to the teacher that I have overburdened the text with Spanish words, I want to say that I have used them freely because I think every American child should have some knowledge of Spanish. Our colonies and our commerce, especially that so soon to be directed through the Panama Canal, alike demand this. The South is already requiring the study of Spanish in some of its public schools. Aside from its utility, Spanish forms a delightful gateway into a new world lying at our very threshold.

Mexico is our nearest really foreign country—as full of color and as fascinating as any country overseas. It is our nearest republic also, and first cousin, so to speak, to Cuba, whom we have known and befriended ever since the Spanish War. We should become better and more amicably acquainted with our neighbor Mexico.

The Life of Little People of Other Countries

Holland Stories

By *Mary E. Smith*, of the Froebel School, Chicago.

Taking little stories of Dutch child life in which the home interests and unique industries of Holland are cleverly associated. In the making of wooden shoes, of cheese, the growing of tulips, the digging of peat, the work of the windmills and canals, the little American will find much to delight and interest him.

Illustrations by *Bonnibel Butler* with 12 full pages in color and 58 line drawings. Cloth.

Child Life in Many Lands

By *H. Avis Perdue*, of the Chicago Normal School, and *Florence E. LaVictoire*, formerly head of the Primary Work, University Elementary School, University of Chicago.

Little tales in which the life, occupations, and national dress of foreign children are the features of importance. Folk stories enrich the narrative, while illustrations of foreign games and toys, together with dramatic and constructive work, give a vivid impression of child life in the most interesting countries of the world. A great favorite with little people.

Many half-tone illustrations. Cloth, 160 pages. Price, 25 cents.

Eskimo Stories

By *Mary E. Smith*, of the Froebel School, Chicago.

Full of movement and the snap of the northern air. Hunting, fishing, and the outdoor sports of the snowbound people and their sturdy little sons are vividly pictured. The strange birds and animals, and the fact that all this is characteristic of part of our own country, makes the little book doubly attractive.

Illustrated with 17 full-page and 77 text illustrations in half-tones by *Howard V. Brown*. Cloth, 189 pages. Price, 40 cents.

Send for Full List of Readers

RAND McNALLY & COMPANY
EDUCATIONAL PUBLISHERS

CHICAGO   NEW YORK